THE SOMALI DECEPTION

EPISODE II

DANIEL ARTHUR SMITH

The Somali Deception Episode II
Copyright © 2010-14 Daniel Arthur Smith
All rights reserved Holt Smith ltd
Second Edition
Cover Design and Formatting by Daniel Arthur Smith
Edited by Crystal Watanabe

Published by Holt Smith Limited
ISBN: 0988649349
ISBN-13: 978-0-9886493-4-7

Also Written by Daniel Arthur Smith

The Cameron Kincaid Adventures
The Cathari Treasure
The Somali Deception

The Literary Fiction Series
The Potter's Daughter
Opening Day: A Short Story

The Horror Series
Agroland

~*~

For Susan, Tristan, & Oliver, as all things are.
&
To all of the others that choose to use crayons to color
their rainbows.

~*~

.

EPISODE II

CHAPTER 20
SHELA VILLAGE, LAMU

Nikos' frantic blubbering had driven Cameron out of the suite. He stood alone on the veranda watching the Lamu dhows glide by, the tall full single sails lifting the crafts forward. The ageless sailboats brought him a soldier's zen. Then the commotion to his back subtly dulled. Cameron sensed someone was physically blocking the chatter. He decided to acknowledge the friend at his back. "Graceful, isn't she?" he said. "The way the captain maneuvers that giant lateen sail as effortlessly as a jib."

"Like a photo," said Alastair from behind.

Alastair might have stood in the doorway the whole of the afternoon, hesitant to disturb Cameron. With his friends acknowledgement he sauntered to the edge of the veranda.

The two brown glass bottles Alastair held by the necks were perspiring. The hotel suite interior was far cooler then the veranda by contrast, yet nowhere near as comforting as the quieter adjacent space. Cameron had not said much to Alastair, or anyone else, since they arrived in Lamu. Eazy and Isaac had handled the logistics of docking the Kalinihta and securing transportation to the Peponi Hotel. Cameron

1

did not need to say much as everything had gone according to plan. Well, almost everything. The primary goal of the mission was to liberate Christine, yet she had not even been at Abbo's compound. Christine had been moved by the warlord days prior.

As if to himself, Cameron said, "They look a lot like the jolly-boats up in the gulf."

"Lamu dhows are jihazi, similar to the jalibut," said Alastair.

"Jihazi? Doesn't that mean..."

"It's a Persian word for ship, I think."

Cameron allowed himself some levity and let out a slight grunt. Alastair offered him one of the brown bottles, "Here, Charlie dropped a few of these by before he went to check on the crew. They're cold." He shrugged, "Well, sort of."

Cameron held the beer up. On the label was a black stencil of an elephant head. "Finest Quality Lager, eh?"

"Try it, Tusker is pretty good. Best you'll get here in Lamu, anyway."

"What does this mean on the label? Bia yangu, Nchi yangu."

"Swahili," said Alastair, "it means, 'my beer, my country.'"

Cameron drank from the brown bottle and let the cold fizz down his throat, letting out a satisfying sigh.

"I told you it wasn't bad," said Alastair.

"Hmm. Thanks," said Cameron. "I was meaning to tell ya, for being out of service, that was a quite maneuver you and Ari pulled on the chopper, despite the rocket."

"Oh, the rocket man. Well, we tag rhino that way," Alastair wobbled his head to the side and back and then sipped his lager, "and the odd poacher."

"The odd poacher?"

Alastair raised his Tusker, "Conservation. I noted you still handle yourself quite well."

Cameron raised his Tusker in return, "Vive la Légion."

Exiting the suite behind them, Pepe added, "The Legion is our strength."

Cameron and Alastair allowed themselves to smile for a moment. Pepe and Isaac joined them on the veranda. Pepe's mere presence reminded Cameron all too quickly of the dread of the day.

"Nikos is talking," said Pepe. His eyes were dark and drawn in.

"What is he saying?" asked Alastair.

Isaac spoke for Pepe, "He is saying the Volunteer National Coast Guard kidnapped him and Christine to leverage his father."

Cameron arched one brow, dropped the other, then twisted his head slowly away from the Lamu dhows, toward Isaac and Pepe, "He said what?"

Isaac continued, "Abbo Mohammed was attempting to leverage Demetrius into increased protection of his shipping fleet."

"So this wasn't merely a ransom. He told you two this?" asked Cameron.

"No, no," said Pepe. "Nikos finally reached his father directly and was quite loud when he spoke to him. We could not help to overhear his yammering." Pepe shook his head.

"Tell me about it," said Cameron.

"Anyway," Pepe locked eyes with Cameron, "Demetrius is apparently paying the Coast Guard to allow passage, and whatever that amount is, Abbo decided it should be more."

Isaac walked to the edge of the veranda next to Alastair, "That explains why the Kalinihta was never officially reported missing. This was a business maneuver from the beginning."

Pepe's gaze was still locked, "A mistake that Abbo will not live long to regret."

"You told me you took out Abbo's son," said Isaac. "That is no small thing."

3

"That is nothing at all," said Pepe.

"Not with these people," said Isaac. "I know he has your sister, but I'm telling you that for men like Abbo Mohammed, the death of a son by another's hand is a catalyst for a Godob, a Somali blood feud. And let me further tell you that all of these clans were established and perpetuated by blood vendettas going back hundreds of years. They live and breathe this. Abbo may be looking for us already."

"Let him come," said Pepe. "He should have thought of such consequences before he took the Kalinihta."

"I'm sure he did and this was nowhere on his radar," said Alastair. "If what Nikos is saying is true, Abbo never meant to harm him. He was flexing old school tribal muscle. I don't think he ever meant to harm anybody. I mean, bloody hell, we found Nikos with his son in a luxury apartment."

"From Abbo's perspective," said Isaac, "his son was killed by a hit squad."

"Isaac's right," said Alastair, "he'll be seeking some bloody twisted flavor of Somali vengeance."

"Then we need to hit first," said Cameron. "Alastair, do you think we can get Stratos on board for more financing?"

"I don't see why not. He's a pretty honorable fellow, perhaps he can get Abbo to simply hand her over," said Alastair.

"I doubt that is going to happen now that Abbo is less one son," said Cameron. "If Isaac is right, then Abbo may be under the impression Stratos himself offed the kid. Pepe, can your contact back in Montreal put us back in touch with Dada?"

"I don't know. I will make the call," said Pepe.

"Why would you want to contact Dada?" asked Isaac.

"We may need some additional connections and intel to hit Abbo and if we're doing Dada a favor, he can do us one."

"That's a dangerous game," said Isaac.

"I game we're already playing, Isaac," said Cameron, "and it's too late for Pepe and I to quit. Pepe, do you suppose your contact would know where to find Abbo?"

"Perhaps, but I doubt they are that informed," said Pepe.

"If not, I have another friend close by," said Cameron.

"Here in Kenya?" asked Alastair.

"Here in Lamu."

CHAPTER 21
SHELA VILLAGE, LAMU

Maggie Soze began life as a socialite and then, after finding her way through the world, found herself in West Africa married to a lodge owner she affectionately nicknamed Tarzan. When the marriage ended, she parlayed her experience and connections into a career in freelance journalism. Cameron had become acquainted with Maggie in New York. When stateside, she was a frequent guest of Cameron's restaurant Le Dragon Vert. Maggie had moxie, something Cameron appreciated. She was as likely to order a rock glass of scotch as a glass of wine.

"It's like we're on a boat," said Maggie, "floating right through the channel along with the dhows."

"Yeah," said Cameron. "The suite I'm in is recessed behind the beach and lawn, no air flow. I think there is actually a breeze here."

Maggie eased her eyes shut, tilted her head back, and inhaled deeply through her nose. "I do believe there is."

Maggie slowly brought her head forward and opened her pool blue eyes into a fixed lock on Cameron's. "You know I love the Peponi. You picked a great hotel. The food here is outstanding. Is that what brought the Dragon

Chef?"

Cameron laughed. "No, though I am a bit hungry. What do you suggest?"

Maggie relaxed her gaze. She slid her turtle shell glasses over the bridge of her nose and reached for the one sheet menu. "Well, let's see what's on special today." She peeked over the rim of her glasses. "The Peponi is not Le Dragon Vert but still pretty good." She veered her attention back toward the menu, "Oh yes, you'll love the prawns."

"Right, I read about them in the New York Times."

"Is that how you heard about this place? I have to say I was surprised when Claude called me."

"Yes, I did read about the Peponi in the New York Times but no, that is not why I am here. Actually, a friend made the arrangements for us."

"Us?" The corner of Maggie's mouth curled up mischievously.

"Us as in a group of friends," said Cameron. "Men. We were in Laikipia and..."

"Oh, and you wanted to get to the coast. I get it. I can't be land locked too long either. There's nothing like a seafront stroll through Shela. Did you know this is a world heritage site? UNESCO." Maggie arched her eyebrows and then removed her glasses, holding them away from her in the air for a moment to inspect, and then, finding no flaw, she set them on the table.

"I was not aware of that," said Cameron.

"That's why there are no cars. Have you been on the seafront when the fishermen bring in the afternoon catch?"

"No, why?"

"Quite a spectacle, cats by the herds show up."

"You don't say."

Maggie sat back in her chair and straightened her back. "Spit it out. What's up?"

Cameron sighed, then furrowed his brow. "Remember that article you wrote a while back on the kidnappings near here?"

"Hmm, the Manda island abductions across the channel. How could I forget? After I wrote that article I had to watch my back, as did every other journalist. Various mzungu and wazungu around Lamu—"

"Mzungu and wazungu?"

"Foreigners and whites, Swahili, dear," Maggie arched her brows again and nonchalantly looked to either side of the table for eavesdroppers. "I was threatened more than once by foreigners and whites with business interests in the tourist sector, and in one case I was physically assaulted because I wrote that magazine article."

"You were physically assaulted?"

"Well, I wasn't beat up. I was doused with a bucket of ice water. Kind of refreshing in a hot place like this, actually. The intent was there, though. Hey, I just wrote the article and the Associated Press picked it up. No fault of mine if there is no security over on Manda. Tourist cancellations started coming in way before I wrote a story about the pirate-slash-tourist kidnappings in Kenya. I mean they have three police patrol boats that never leave the dock because the money that's earmarked for hotelier security ends up in some politician's pocket."

"Really?"

"Oh yeah, this place is paradise but there is a reason they call the government serekali."

"Swahili again, and why is that?" asked Cameron.

"As I understand, the Swahili words siri and kali mean secret and fierce."

Cameron nodded his head. "And the pirates?"

"Probably no different than the rest of them, taking payoffs. Those abductions were just some strays, off the reservation, if you will. As were the other abductions you have heard about. The female journalist that was held and raped a few years ago, and the aid workers. Thugs took those poor people, the equivalent of teenage street gangs. Those gangs are not the real power up there. There is a lot more going on."

"Like Abbo Mohammed?"

Maggie's eyes lit up, "Wow, now we cut to the quick. You picked a hell of a name to drop."

Cameron let his smile go subtly coy, "So is he a local player or what?"

Maggie sat silent for a moment, smiling at Cameron.

"You're sizing me up," said Cameron.

"You're a chef," said Maggie.

"Among other things," said Cameron. "So off the record, what can you tell me about Abbo?"

"Off the record?"

"All off the record. I like to keep private."

"Okay, I'll play. So, Abbo Mohammed is 'the' local player. If you did not know, he runs a little group not far north from here called the Volunteer National Coast Guard, and that little group, like some other groups up the coast, has a nasty reputation as a band of pirates. But they're not."

"They're not?" asked Cameron.

"No, they are not. Well, they are and they aren't. Semantics."

"What are you saying?"

"Their designation as pirates is a bit of a misnomer. A better word might be..."

Maggie pursed her lips pondering a word choice.

"Warlord, militia," said Cameron.

"Cartel," said Maggie. "Their reputation as pirates has actually helped them in the past, creates this picture of a rag tag group of unwashed men in rags tearing around in little wooden skiffs. Detracts from what they actually are."

"And what is that?"

"The strong arm of the northern horn of Africa. They control shipping in the Indian and western Pacific oceans, parts of Indonesia and South America now too, and they run grift across all of these waters."

"Grift?"

"That's their big money. All of those yachts, ships, and freighters that are picked up bearing precarious flags, a good

9

portion of them are prearranged insurance scams or illegal cargo transfers under the guise of a siege. There's protection money for the giant fisheries, and Lord knows what they're dumping in the waters out there."

"That sounds like a lot," said Cameron.

"It is. As pirates, they're documented around 120 million US dollars a year. I hear the real numbers are more like three billion."

"Whoa."

"Yeah," said Maggie, "probably still a lowball. It's never where you see it."

"I guess not. No wonder they have such a strong foothold."

"They're allowed a foothold because they're suppressing Al Qaeda in the Arabian Peninsula. The cartels are clan driven and even though Al Shabaab is predominantly intertwined, the cartels are the decision makers. As long as they're funded, they are in charge," said Maggie.

"Al Shabaab means the youth," said Cameron.

"And the clans are run by the elders."

"And Abbo is an elder."

"Technically a sheikh maybe, I don't know. He is the cartel elder."

"Where can I find him?" asked Cameron.

"You want to find Abbo Mohammed?"

"Do you know where he is?"

"Sure I know. He's not that hard to find. He holds up where all the shady billion dollar deals take place. You'll find Abbo Mohammed in Dubai. What do you plan to do, march in and cook him something?"

"You'd be surprised," said Cameron. "Actually, we have a friend to help us make contact, Ibrahim—"

"Ibrahim Dada!"

"You know the name?"

"Don't be fresh. You should be real careful of the friends you are making lately."

"I can use the help, so right now I am going with the old saying 'the enemy of my enemy is my friend,'" said Cameron.

Maggie leaned back and peered into Cameron's eyes, "I hope you know what you're doing. The old saying you should be concerned with is 'with friends like that, who needs enemies?'"

CHAPTER 22
PARIS, FIFTEEN YEARS BEFORE

Christine entered the small galley kitchen and agilely slipped her naked body behind Cameron as he buttered golden chunks of the egg-fried bread he had prepared from the remnants of last evening's loaf. She wrapped her arms tightly around him, rested her cheek on his upper back, and made a warm purring sound. Cameron felt her nakedness through his thin cotton shirt. Her warmth prompted his chest to flex as she squeezed.

"Bonjour, l'amour," said Cameron, his voice soft and sing song.

"I cannot believe you were up so early," said Christine, her eyes still closed, heavy with sleep. "What time is it?" she nuzzled further into Cameron's shoulder muscles.

"I did not want to wake you until breakfast was ready," said Cameron.

"Did you make coffee?"

"Yes, and it's not that early."

"No? I do not believe you." Christine softly nudged her head deeper into Cameron's shoulder. "We should go back to bed."

Cameron smiled contently and began to place the

bread onto a plate, "What happened to going out today? Remember? A walk by the river, a gallery, maybe a trip to the country."

"Yes, yes," said Christine. "I want to do those things today." She lifted her head and tugged Cameron's shirt, turning him toward her. "That would be so nice. To have you for myself today." She lifted her arms up over his shoulders and pulled herself close to him. He met her with a kiss. First a long one and then two fast smooches. Her lids sprung open, her green eyes lively and jubilant, awaken by his touch.

"Whoa," said Cameron. "Where did that come from?"

"You remind me, I love you." Christine grabbed a piece of the bread from the plate and the jar of jam from the counter, "First you must feed me. I am so hungry." Her eyes and mouth both went wide as she tore off a chunk of the bread. Mouth full, cheeks puffed, she smiled at Cameron, and then slipped past him toward the table.

Cameron set the plate of egg battered bread on the table along with some goat cheese, honey, and the coffee. When he sat, Christine was already voraciously under way with breakfast. Cameron laughed and Christine returned a full smile. Cameron bit into a piece of bread and then chuckled. He placed his hand over his mouth.

"What?" asked Christine.

Cameron pointed at the corner of his mouth as if he were Christine's mirror. She put a finger near her lip, "Oh," she said, and wiped away a splotch of honey. Cameron's smile did not fade. Christine lifted her brows in question. "And um," Cameron tapped his chest. She looked down, "Oh," she said. She gave him a toothy bread-filled grin. Then with her pinky she dabbed at the drops of honey that had drizzled upon her breasts, rubbing them into her flesh.

"I guess they were hungry," said Cameron.

"I cannot help myself, this food is so good. I did not know I had spices on my shelves."

"Only cinnamon and sugar."

Her eyes went wide again, her head wobbled side to side, "Only cinnamon and sugar? I would not know the first thing to do. You, my love, are in the wrong line of work."

Cameron took in a slow breath. The flat was shielded from the morning light by shadow and curtains of lace, yet Christine's green eyes shone bright. To him, she embodied beauty. Her physical beauty was undeniable, her long chestnut hair wildly flowing over her bare shoulders. No man could resist the charms of perfectly formed pert breasts slathered in shining droplets of honey. Certainly, they shared lust. To Cameron though, Christine also held the beauty of innocence, happily rocking side to side as she ate, now humming a song, most likely one of her own creation. Most of all Cameron believed—wanted to believe—that Christine did not know the work he did when he was away from her. When Cameron was by her side, that man was someone else.

"Cameron," said Christine.

"*Oui, l'amour,*" said Cameron.

Christine tilted her head to the side and gazed into Cameron's eyes. He could become lost in those eyes and never go back to Corsica, to the regiment. Maybe one day.

"Today," said Christine. "I want to look at puppies."

"You want to look at puppies?"

"Yes, puppies. One of the girls has this beautiful new labrador. She says he is a chocolate Lab. He is very cute and keeps her company when…"

Christine shifted her eyes down to the table and bit off a small piece of bread. She chewed the piece more slowly than needed. Cameron waited for her to finish her sentence and when she did not he prompted her, "When…?"

Christine sighed and then sat upright in her chair, still peering at the table. "I do not want to think bad thoughts today. I need you to go with me to find a puppy to keep me company for when you are not here." She slid her eyes up from the table to meet Cameron's again, at the same time grasping his fingers into hers. Playfully pleading, she said, "Would you do that, Cameron? Would you go with me to find a chocolate Lab puppy?"

Cameron leaned forward and responded in the guise of a playful lover, "Oui, of course I will go with you to find a chocolate Lab puppy."

Christine lurched forward and planted a kiss on Cameron, wrapping her hand around his head so that he could not escape. When she sat back into her chair, the toothy smile returned to her face. "Fabulous," she placed her hands flatly together, "I know just the place in the country, and then we can have a picnic."

Seeing Christine so satisfied and joyful, Cameron could not help feeling the same. To simply make her happy made him happy. Cameron again imagined a world where he could easily stay here in Paris.

Again Christine's face became serious, "Cameron."

"Oui, l'amour."

"Thank you for being here with me."

"Where else would I be?" Cameron placed his arm across the table and Christine rested her hand in his.

Christine smiled. Then a brief moment later, "Cameron."

"Oui, l'amour."

"Thank you for making this lovely breakfast." Christine offered her cup to Cameron, and then sheepishly asked, "May I have more coffee?"

CHAPTER 23
AL MARMOOM CAMEL RACETRACK, DUBAI

From his seat in the grandstand, the stringy twelve year old flung his naked arm down toward the starting gate pit. From the sea of owners, trainers, and entourages packed tightly behind the twenty-three painted camels, the boy singled out one man. "That's him in the full body thobe and ghutra."

"Very funny, little one," said Pepe. "They all are wearing thobes and ghutras."

"We're wearing thobes and ghutras," said Cameron. "Can you be more specific?"

In his tattered desert tanned t-shirt and matching light denim pants, the boy, Rehan, was the only person on the grandstand not wearing a thobe and ghutra. The boy shrugged the shoulder of protruding arm, "You said you wanted the younger man from the Kingdom."

"Yes," said Pepe.

"He is there in the white thobe and red checkered ghutras." The boy pressed his arm out farther, wagging his hand toward the man. "There behind the red painted camel

16

with the green robot. The one with the number nine on the side, talking to the tall bald man."

"Yeah," said Pepe. "I see." He fixed his eyes on the man the boy had described, the only one of the small Arab horde to wear a red-checkered ghutra, was close to his trainer, passionately gesturing toward the length of the track. "Yes, that's him." Pepe tilted his head close to Cameron, "And look who is with him, our friend from the London garage."

"That's the man from London, all right," said Cameron. "Looks like he is stepping away. Good."

Cameron slipped his hand into his thobe and retrieved a bright pink folded note revealing a picture of a hawk and the number one hundred. He held the paper toward the boy.

Rehan's eyes widened. He snapped for the money.

"Hold on," said Cameron, lifting the bill above the boy's reach. "This dirham is yours as well as the others we promised." He handed Rehan the bill.

"And the rest?" asked Rehan.

"First I need you to go down there and tell the Saudi that two Frenchmen are here to see him."

"But you speak English."

"And so do you," said Pepe, "so what?"

Rehan nodded and scurried down the grandstand toward the camel pit, his dusted shirt and trousers blending into the tan sand and shadow below the grandstand. He wove his way through the crowded staging area, disappeared, reappeared, and then popped up in front of the man. The Saudi, elegant in his pristine white thobe, froze mid-gesture of explanation to his trainer of how he saw the race that was to be run, and then tilted his head down to the urchin pauper boy before him. Rehan held his clasped hands up to the man and then swung back around toward the grandstands and pointed with the same overextended arm and waggling hand he had used a moment before. The Saudi fixed his gaze near Cameron and Pepe, his eyes searching.

"Smile and wave," said Cameron as he subtly raised his hand. Pepe did the same.

Having seen their signal, the Saudi smiled, slightly bowed his head, and waved back. He held up his hand with the palm upwards and all of the fingers together and made a small movement with his wrist to signify he was almost finished and then he turned back to his trainer.

"Watch this," said Cameron.

"He will not leave until he has a reward," said Pepe referring to the boy, still standing in the Saudi's shadow. The Saudi appeared surprised to realize the boy was still there. He said something to Rehan, and then attempted to return to the trainer.

"Not that easy," said Cameron, and he was correct, as the Saudi next gave Rehan something out of the leather pouch. Only then did the boy disappear again into the crowd.

"I don't know about this guy," said Cameron.

"Considering he is friends with Abbo, that should tell you enough. Then again, he is willing to betray him to us, so..."

"Even that makes me queasy. I mean, we're here for the morning races. Only sheikhs race in the morning and this fella owns a camel."

"A lipstick wearing camel."

"I think they are all wearing lipstick. Anyway, if this guy is a Royal Saud why is he willing to talk to us? What's the deal between him and Abbo anyway?" asked Cameron.

"He owes Abbo money," said Pepe. "A lot of it."

"This fella appears to be loaded."

"All appearances. My contact tells me this man is way down on the Saudi food chain, barely on the radar. He is in hock over his head. That is why he will talk to us. We erase Abbo and—"

"His debt is erased," finished Cameron.

"Voila."

"Must be quite a debt."

The boy shot up from the bottom the grandstands. "He is coming. He says he has to be fast as the race is to begin."

"I'm sure he has a lot riding on that little robot," said Cameron.

"Excuse me, sir?" asked Rehan.

"Wagered, I am sure he has a lot wagered."

"Oh, no. I am sure he does not."

"Why is that?"

"Gambling is strictly forbidden."

"Then why is he so pumped up?"

"Oh, the prizes are great. A luxury SUV, a luxury car, and yesterday someone won twelve luxury cars. And in the morning race, if you win, or place in the top three, another sheikh will surely purchase your camel for great riches."

"Bingo," sad Pepe. "He wants the prize money. A passive way to stay liquid."

"Okay, here he comes," said Cameron.

"Run along for now, little one," said Pepe, a fifty-dirham bill already extended. The boy grabbed the bill, then rolled his eyes at Pepe. Pepe began to stand, "Go on, and come back when the race begins."

Rehan scurried back down the grandstand steps the way he had come, circumventing the Saudi along the way. The Saudi raised his arms, scowling as the boy passed around him.

Cameron and Pepe began to rise as the Saudi reached their seats. He waved his hand to gesture they remain seated. The Saudi faced the track, smoothed the length of his thobe, and then without shifting his focus away from his camel, took a seat next to Pepe.

"Ahlan wasahlan," Pepe greeted the Saudi, being sure to mirror the man's mannerism of keeping his attention toward the track and not obligating him to make eye contact.

"Ahlan feek," said the Saudi.

Now that the man was up close, Cameron and Pepe were able to see that the Saudi, as described, was a younger man, perhaps late twenties, with the handsome look of an aristocrat. His face was smooth and his eyes jeweled. Having met this type before, they were able to discern this man was arrogant and spoiled, most likely the flaws that were key to his undoing.

"A fine morning for a camel race," said Pepe in his most congenial manner.

The Saudi's voice betrayed his disdain and disgust for the two men beside him. His eyes remained fixed on his camel down below, "So you are the Frenchmen from Montreal?"

"Oui," said Pepe.

"Have you ever been to a camel race before?"

"No. I cannot say that I have."

"Well, let me tell you. There has not been a good morning for camel racing in years, not since they started wrapping these electronic devices in Arabian cloth and weaving them into the saddlebags. Age old tradition tossed aside for public relations."

"I see. The human jockeys were better?"

"Much better," said the Saudi, and for the first time, he allowed himself to inspect Pepe and Cameron. Then he returned his focus to the red painted camel, "Anyway, I understand you are looking for a mutual friend."

Pepe and Cameron, of course, were not unnerved at this joke of a man and continued to feign interest in the pit below, even in the brief moment the Saudi had turned to them. "Yes," said Pepe, "I was told you would be able tell us where to find this…friend, in Dubai, and more importantly, assist us in getting us close to him."

"You understand correctly."

"So will you do this?" asked Pepe.

"Yes. I will help you, though there are some conditions."

"Conditions? What do you mean?"

"It was made clear to me that your intentions are to kill our friend."

"That may happen," said Pepe.

Cameron slipped his hand into his thobe, wanting to be near his weapon if needed.

"I am good with this. And though your business is not my own, I did have to ask myself why you would want to do such a thing."

"I assure you, our action will serve us both," said Pepe.

The Saudi turned his head and faced Pepe, "Well, I did some digging, and it is like this, Mister Laroque." Pepe took measure of the Saudi's expression. The Saudi continued, "I need to think of my best interest. Were you not to succeed, how do I benefit?"

Pepe, his face calm and voice kind, matched eyes with the Saudi, "We are here to do business. What do you want?"

The Saudi patted Pepe on the leg, "I am glad you understand. I need a small fee. Insurance, if you will."

Pepe's voice drew cold, "How much?"

The Saudi again put his attention on the camel pit, obviously annoyed, "What is he doing now?" The Saudi fruitlessly raised his hand toward his trainer.

Pepe repeated his question again, his voice deeper, "How much?"

The Saudi faced Pepe and this time placed his hand on his shoulder, "The fee will be one million US dollars, Mister Laroque." He then smiled and began to stand.

"That is no small amount," said Pepe.

"No," said the Saudi, "that is the amount, however, that Abbo is offering for information concerning his son. Listen, I have to get down to the track. When I have finished I will return for your answer." The Saudi began to start toward the camel pit then stopped himself. "Oh, there is one more thing."

"Yes," said Pepe.

"Something to help you decide."

"On with it."

"A new woman has been brought into Abbo's harem," said the Saudi. "A woman with chestnut hair and green eyes."

CHAPTER 24
AL MARMOOM CAMEL RACETRACK, DUBAI

Scattered shouts rose to howls and then a collective roar as people began to rise in the grandstands. On every tiered level, those nearest the front massed forward, tightly pressing against each other, folding those at the edge over the railings.

"Would you look at that," said Cameron.

Still a kilometer away, an elongated cloud of dust rapidly rounded the outside turn of the Al Marmoom Camel Racetrack, a rolling haze that covered all except the front-runners of the consolidated pack of painted camels and the pace keeping armada of white four-by-four Land Cruisers. Sporadic bursts of sunlight gleamed off the windscreens of the Land Cruisers that briefly slipped the grasp of the looming dust to shuffle for position. Striding forward at remarkable speed, the camels appeared to hover above the hot desert track—a Fata Morgana, a mirage—the trailing racers obscurely fading in and out of view.

"They are making good time," said Rehan.

"They seem to be running themselves," said Cameron.

From the grandstands, the tiny electronic robot jockeys appeared to be mere colored cloth atop the lean camels' backs.

"They are not," said Rehan.

Cameron flashed a glance to size up the boy, unsure of the response. He decided to go along, "The remotes are in the four-by-fours?"

"Yes, and some of the cameras are on the bonnets."

"The bonnets?"

Rehan gestured, "On the top."

"Right, the people riding rigs on the tops of the Land Cruisers. There are so many."

"I once saw a race with forty SUVs, they will not allow more."

"Too many camels?"

Rehan laughed at Cameron's comment, "No, of course not. The Bedouin will race a hundred camels. The sheikhs race with the SUV. More than forty is too many Land Cruisers."

"Ah," said Cameron.

Pepe leaned into Cameron's ear, "Are you ready?"

Cameron nodded.

"We need to go now, little one," said Pepe. "Take us to where the man's car is parked."

"Can we see the end of the race?" asked Rehan.

Cameron patted the boy's shoulder, "We will watch from the monitors. Let's go while we can."

"This way then," said Rehan, already in motion.

Rehan had a sense of the crowd. He moved through the openings behind and around the large gathered groups, instinctively avoiding the bottlenecks at the stairwell landings and the congested entrance to the interior concession area, where those that had been lining the corridor in wait for the bathrooms were now pushing out toward the track. Cameron and Pepe stayed close behind, choosing to mimic the boy's snakelike maneuvers rather than lose pace and have to awkwardly chase after him. Still,

Cameron and Pepe were grown men and though agile, young boys they were not. Fortunately, the Al Marmoom guests were focused on the last minutes of the race, intoxicated by the elixir of the finish line.

The concession area in the belly of the grandstand was predominantly empty, with the exception of a few men scurrying from the kitchens. Each carried a brass pot of cardamom-infused coffee, fresh brewed for the regal passengers of the four-by-fours about to finish the race. The monitors covering the walls featured the high definition live action of the camels up close, their tongues loosely draping their ears and pasty saliva spewing from their mouths. The small bulk of the robot jockeys on the camels' backs were clearly visible and the attached whips, engaged for the final stretch, could be seen rhythmically striking the rear quarters of the lumbering beasts.

Above the three, the excitement of the crowd began to build.

"It is almost finished," said Rehan.

The roar and movement from above amplified to a thunderous roar in the concrete cavern of the concession space.

Cameron raised his voice, "And then what?"

"As soon as each race finishes, the sheikhs and royals step out of their cars to greet spectators and the people rush to them, eager to congratulate the winners."

"Everyone rushes down?"

"They may all win a prize," said Rehan. "Sometimes the sheikhs are very generous. Like the great Oprah."

A new image dominated all of the monitors, across which flashed first a purple, then an orange, and then a blue-blanketed camel; none of the three belonging to the Saudi. The hollers and applause that had been gradually building now peaked in a raucous crescendo, a final outburst of excitement that expired to a murmur and the unmistakable sound of an exodus from the seating area above.

"This way," said Rehan, leading Cameron and Pepe to

the back of the concession space. Once free from the cavernous echo of the interior, the day drew new calm. Eyes widened and jaws slacked, Cameron and Pepe attempted to refresh their hearing. The space not enclosed by the concession area was used for private parking, which extended to the farther portion of the grandstands and wrapped around to access the racetrack. The palatial back of the grandstands opened out into an oasis of precious green lawn and palm trees, the centerpiece of which was a large, round pool fountain and an aesthetic bridge to the outside parking area beyond.

"I don't think I have ever seen so many Maybachs and Mercedes at once," said Cameron. "This place looks like a dealership."

"Billboard included," said Pepe, referring to the oversized digital monitor mounted above the parked cars.

Rehan was not fazed, "The camel minders wait for their camel to cross the finish line so they can escort him off the track. The trainer will be with the four-by-four, leaving your man to come through here. Everyone else will be trackside with the winners for some time."

"You're sure of that?" asked Cameron.

"His highness Sheikh Mohammed bin Rashid Al Maktoum was a winner today, so he will be greeting admirers. Everyone will be lining up to congratulate him. His highness is very generous."

Pepe smirked, "The number one guy himself. You know, I truly and honestly respect and admire him. From what I hear, on many accounts across sources, he really is a nice person, cares for his people, and for the reputation of his country."

Cameron rolled his eyes, "I'll take note of that."

Rehan reached into his pocket and retrieved a black key fob, "I parked your Mercedes there. That Maybach over there belongs to the man from the Kingdom."

"The white Maybach there?" asked Pepe.

"No," said Rehan. "The black one."

"Okay," said Pepe. He held his hand out for the key fob and the boy pulled his arm away.

"Don't worry," said Cameron. He held two hundred dirham bills up and the boy slapped the key fob into his hand in exchange. Cameron grinned at Pepe. Pepe scowled and then peered up at the monitor.

"What are they smearing all over those camels?" asked Pepe.

"The heads and necks of the three top placers from the race are smeared with saffron paste before being paraded in front of the spectators," said Rehan.

"Saffron?" Pepe glanced back at Cameron, "Saffron is expensive, oui?"

"I believe the winning camels are ceremoniously doused in turmeric," said Cameron, "essentially low quality saffron."

Pepe grunted then shifted his eyes past Cameron's shoulder. The Saudi and his driver, a giant of a man, were walking along the far edge of the parking structure toward the black Maybach. The Saudi was speaking on his mobile phone and had not yet noticed Cameron and Pepe near the concessions entrance. "There he is," said Pepe, "right on time. Good job little one. Get along now."

"Call my mobile if you need anything else," said Rehan, then he slipped past the two men back through the entranceway.

"Call his mobile," muttered Cameron.

"Don't worry, I have his number. Things are different here you know."

Cameron pursed his lip, "I guess, you ready?"

Pepe nodded, "Yeah, let's go."

CHAPTER 25
AL MARMOOM CAMEL RACETRACK, DUBAI

Cameron and Pepe sauntered across the aisle of the parking area to the black Maybach that Rehan had told them belonged to the Saudi. As there were at least three other black Maybachs in this small section of the structure alone, there was a chance that the boy may have been mistaken.

The Saudi and his driver were steps away before they realized that Cameron and Pepe were waiting beside the Maybach to greet them. The Saudi said something into his mobile that they could not hear and then slipped the phone into his bag. He then gazed at Pepe with a closed smile, a smile of contentment and satisfaction.

"Ahlan wasahlan," said the Saudi.

"Ahlan feek," said Pepe.

"I honestly did not think I would see the two of you again so quickly."

"You mentioned you needed an answer after the race," said Pepe.

The Saudi clasped his hands together in front of his chest, "So I did."

Cameron took one half step forward, "How was the race, by the way?"

The corners of the Saudi's mouth dropped. He slowly faced Cameron.

Cameron continued, "I mean, you didn't even place did you?"

The Saudi let both of his eyes briefly rest shut and then reopen, "No, I did not. My robot did not respond accordingly."

"Yeah, funny things, electronics," said Cameron. He reached into his thobe and removed a small object, which he then tossed to the Saudi.

The Saudi opened his clasped hands enough to catch the object, "What is this?"

"Just a piece of electronics."

"I don't understand."

"You see, I know why you are running out of here so quick. I mean, ahead of everyone else." Cameron raised his hand and extended his finger, an insult alone, and then he began to wave his finger, a further insult. "You made a wager, didn't you? And you lost that wager."

"How do you know?" asked the Saudi.

"Oh, I know." Cameron nodded at Pepe. "Tell him."

"He knows," said Pepe.

"You made a huge bet that you cannot cover," said Cameron.

"You do not know what you are talking about. Gambling is forbidden here," said the Saudi.

"Maybe so, maybe so."

"No maybe. Forbidden, I am no fool."

"I have a feeling that you are in a position to make a deal and give us Abbo," said Cameron, "and that little piece of electronics tells me so."

"What are you saying? What is this?" The Saudi held the small piece up, a black plastic cube with small pins protruding from one side.

"That there is the device, or like the device that tells

me you are in trouble. Or maybe that is the device or like the device that tells your camel he is in trouble."

The Saudi's eyes now pierced Cameron. "Did you tamper with my robot?"

"Doesn't matter, you lost and you owe and we are the only friends you have," said Cameron.

Pepe smiled at the Saudi, "What do you say we take a moment. Things have changed from half an hour ago. Our mutual friend will not be happy with you. Maybe you see things our way now."

The Saudi closed his eyes briefly again, "Perhaps you're right. Meet me tonight." From his bag, he retrieved a card. "Here, call this number this evening and I will tell you where I can meet you."

"That's not necessary," said Cameron. "All we need to know is how to get to Abbo and your problems and our problems are solved."

The Saudi composed himself and for the first time signaled his driver to step forward.

"Call me," said the Saudi. "We will eat, start over."

Cameron took another step forward, "I would rather—"

The Saudi threw up his hand in a gesture for Cameron to stop and the driver slipped his hand into his thobe and revealed the top half of a submachine gun.

Cameron threw his hands up and stepped back, "Okay, okay. Dinner then."

"Dinner then," said the Saudi.

Cameron and Pepe stepped from behind the Maybach to allow the Saudi into his car without further discussion. The luxury car backed out of the parking space.

"What was that electronic thing you gave him?" asked Pepe.

The car slowly moved past the two men. Cameron and Pepe smiled, offered a gentle wave, and then bowed their heads at the dark tinted windows of the Maybach.

"Part of the electric eye sensor from the concession

entrance. I figured that would throw him."

"Clever. I believe you succeeded."

"Thank you, I think so too," said Cameron, he lifted the key fob Rehan had given him and tapped a button. The taillights of the Mercedes flashed.

"You know," said Pepe. "He is going to try to make a deal with Abbo to trade us for his debt."

"Well, he thinks he is," said Cameron. "We are about to talk him out of doing such a foolish thing."

CHAPTER 26
AL MARMOOM CAMEL RACETRACK, DUBAI

Cameron let the Mercedes idle in the shaded entrance of the parking structure as he and Pepe watched the Saudi's Maybach follow the service road out of the Al Marmoom Camel Racetrack. When the Maybach reached the first grandstand near the complex edge, Cameron accelerated into the sunlight.

Pepe leaned over the front seat, "How far do you want to follow him?"

"Not far," said Cameron. "Clear of the racetrack, before the Dubai Highway."

"How about that stadium over there, behind us? The entrance is on the left, right before the Highway 77 ramp."

Cameron glanced into the rearview mirror. "You want to get him into that large stadium back there?"

"That's the Sevens rugby stadium. The place was empty when we came in."

"Sounds good," said Cameron. "Hold tight." They turned toward the Alain-Dubai road. "This will only take a minute." The engine revved as Cameron punched the pedals, shifting to a higher gear.

To reach Dubai Highway, Highway 77, vehicles turned right out of the racetrack complex onto the Al Marmoom service road, traveled the opposite direction of the highway a few hundred meters, and then turned to cross the parallel two-lane Alain-Dubai road, properly Highway 66, to reverse back.

The Maybach would be turning onto Highway 66 in seconds and driving directly back toward the Mercedes. If Cameron's timing was correct, he would be turning right onto the service road at the precise time the Maybach exited, giving him the opportunity to catch up before his quarry turned back. Cameron's timing was almost always correct. He evaded out of habit rather than necessity. Providing an evasive pursuit out on this stretch of road really did not matter. The black Mercedes Cameron was driving could have been any one of the many from the parking structure or on the highway. The only vehicles more numerous than the luxury sedans this far from the city were the myriad of high-end four-by-fours.

In less than a minute, the Mercedes was on Highway 66 behind the Maybach and closing fast.

"Are we clear?" asked Pepe.

"Not another car on the road," said Cameron.

"This will be like the Algarve job then?"

"Right, I will pinch the quarter and you—"

"Close the deal."

"Vive la Légion," said Cameron.

Pepe responded, "The Legion is our strength."

The driver of the Maybach would not know what was happening until it was too late, if he ever realized at all. Cameron's years of training and experience made the deadly task effortless in execution, and essentially that is what the maneuver was, an execution. In a country notorious for reckless speeding, the driver of the Maybach most likely took no notice of the black Mercedes rapidly approaching from behind to pass on his right. He probably could have responded better than to jerk the steering wheel to the left when the black car cut him off by too quickly moving into his lane, had his head not been removed from his body by two gun blasts from the other vehicle's rear window. Odds are he never saw Pepe or the muzzle flash, both appearing in the brief instance that the corner of the Maybach's windscreen aligned with the back seat of the Mercedes.

Cameron was surprised as well. The maneuver anticipated bulletproof glass and was meant to jar the driver into a wheelhouse jerk of the steering wheel. Despite the overkill, the Maybach went exactly where Cameron and Pepe had wanted, a billiard ball to Pepe's bullet cue, right into the stadium side pocket. One thing that Cameron and Pepe had not anticipated was that there was no exit to the Sevens rugby stadium from their far lane. This portion of the Alain-Dubai road was a proper multi-directional highway split by a median. Fortunately, there were no dividers of any kind, so coupled with luck, the Maybach made the journey across the median, over the other lane, and onto the Sevens Stadium service road.

Cameron spun the Mercedes around and crossed the median to follow their target. The Maybach traveled a few hundred meters toward the stadium, eventually slowed, and then finally came to a full stop.

"He's going to run," said Pepe, again leaning over the front seat, his handgun dangling in his clutch.

"They always run," said Cameron. "That was an amazing shot."

A light grunt was the only sound Pepe made.

Mere meters away the rear door of the Maybach flung open and the Saudi awkwardly poured himself out of the car.

"There he is," said Cameron. Cameron tapped the accelerator to shorten the tedious task of apprehending the Saudi.

"Oui," said Pepe, "please make this quick. He is tripping over his thobe. Very pitiful."

The Mercedes swerved up next to the Saudi. Pepe swung open the rear door in front of the man. The Saudi, his pristine white thobe now sprayed bright crimson, threw up both of his arms and stumbled backward, then dropped to his knees.

"Calm down," said Pepe.

The Saudi veered up at Pepe and then projected thick vomit onto the asphalt.

"Oh, that is disgusting," said Pepe. "Listen, I promise you I will not shoot. See? I give the gun to my friend."

Cameron reached up behind his head to take the handgun from Pepe.

"Are you sure?" asked the Saudi, his face also speckled with bright red spatter.

"Very sure, now get in before I change my mind."

The Saudi moved toward the Mercedes, slowly at first, and then scampered into the backseat with Pepe, perchance for safety.

"Excuse me," said Pepe, as he reached over the man to close the door, trying not to rest his own thobe against the blood on the Saudi's.

"We all in?" asked Cameron.

"Oui," said Pepe. "Uh, take us around the back of the stadium where we can talk in private." He furrowed his brow to the Saudi, "Relax, we are only going up here a bit. Maybe we should buckle you in."

CHAPTER 27
SEVENS RUGBY STADIUM, DUBAI

Cameron glanced into the Mercedes' rearview mirror. The Saudi had undergone a metamorphosis. Caustic and threatening at the track, he had become something altogether different.

The Saudi rested with his eyes closed, letting his face and jaw go completely lax. He appeared ill, his facial pallor accentuated by brilliant crimson spatter. He drew in a deep breath through his nose that did not give rise to his chest, his body rejecting the cooler air of the Mercedes. His full upper body quivered.

"He's going to wretch again," said Cameron.

"No," said Pepe in a soft voice. "No, he is calming. Go ahead and breathe."

The Saudi began to rapidly mouth some words, a mantra, a prayer, again and again, silently at first, then at a whisper. From the front seat, Cameron could make out the mantra clearly, "A-ozu billahi mena shaitaan Arrajeem, A-ozu billahi mena shaitaan Arrajeem." Cameron understood Arabic; it was a Muslim phrase, mainly used when one was feeling unsafe or when scared by something. Roughly translated, the phrase meant, 'I seek refuge in Allah from the cursed Satan.' Pepe also understood the meaning of this phrase. The overall meaning was that the Saudi was right where they wanted him.

In a still soothing tone, Pepe spoke again, "You pray for Allah to be with you." Pepe nodded his head, "The great Allah is with you. My friend and I, we are not the cursed Satan. Do not feel unsafe, do not feel scared, try to relax."

The Saudi opened his eyes, large and round, wanting to escape Pepe. "Relax?" he said. "You could have killed me. You killed Faheem! You could have killed me!"

"Whoa, whoa, 'could have' is not the same as did," said Pepe. "I did not wish to kill Faheem."

"Then why did you shoot him in the head?"

"My goal was to scare him off the road. You did not have bulletproof glass. Who does not have bulletproof glass? I cannot believe you did not have bulletproof glass." Pepe lifted his hands in frustration, sighed, clasped his hands, and then continued, "Very unnecessary, you know, *we* have bulletproof glass. This is only a rental."

The Saudi sank into his seat, now appearing more a boy and less a man. The blood sprayed upon him was already beginning to dry in the cool air of the Mercedes.

Cameron found a loading dock behind the stadium and pulled the Mercedes down the concrete ramp. The Mercedes lowered from the surrounding view. He stepped out of the car, closed the door, and inspected the bay. With the loading bay doors closed, they were essentially parked in a concrete box. Above, Cameron spied two cameras. Someone could be watching. They would need to be prudent. He walked to the rear door of the Mercedes and pulled the handle.

The Saudi did not move.

"Go on," said Pepe from inside the car. "Out of the car."

The Saudi sat stolid, staring at the headrest in front of him per chance Cameron and the open door would disappear.

Pepe's voice softened further, his always-calming deep accent possessed an additional quality of assurance and he placed his hand onto the Saudi's, "It is okay, Taufiq."

In a meek voice, Taufiq replied, "You are going to shoot me now."

"No, my friend," said Pepe soothingly, "I promised I will not shoot you."

"Then your friend will," Taufiq closed his eyes again. "A-ozu billahi mena shaitaan Arrajeem, A-ozu billahi mena—"

"Now, now. Do not be silly," said Pepe. "Neither of us will shoot you. We need your help. We only want to talk to you."

"Really?"

"Really. Now, let's go."

"Okay," said Taufiq. He placed his arms by his sides to upright his torso and then swung his feet out of the Mercedes, standing as tall and elegantly as he could to regain stature, to save face. He spread his fingers wide and smoothed the front of his no longer pristine thobe and then, without looking down, indifferently tried to brush away any of the dried rust colored blood that may have gotten onto his hands. Cameron stood tall as well, respectfully holding the door for the Saudi as he exited the Mercedes and performed his little ritual. Pepe opened his own door on the other side of the Mercedes and then slowly joined the two, giving the Saudi a further chance to compose himself.

His back to Cameron, Taufiq peered forward as if he could see through or over the top of the ramp to the vast parking area and immensely vaster desert beyond.

"So," said Pepe, approaching Taufiq from the rear of the Mercedes. "Can we now speak?"

"Abbo will kill me for telling you his location."

"You are telling us Abbo's location so that we can kill him. Abbo will not be a threat to you."

"And," said Cameron. Startled by a voice from behind,

Taufiq spun on his heel to face them both. Cameron was still standing behind the open rear door, leaning forward on one arm. Cameron continued, "Your debts will be clear. Abbo will not have sold them. Your slate will be clean."

Taufiq backed away from between the two. He moved toward the sidewall of the loading bay, and then spun on his heel again. He placed a hand flat against the concrete and then faced them, "How do I know you can pull this off?"

Cameron dropped and shook his head chuckling, then gazed up at Taufiq, "Well, you had a back seat view of what we did out there moments ago and let me tell you, we were not really trying."

Taufiq drooped his head, "Oh, yes." He raised his eyes to Pepe, "Not even trying?"

Pepe, sauntering toward Taufiq, shook his head, "Not really."

"Okay, okay. Yes, I guess that is right." Suddenly pensive, the Saudi stared at the ground, placed his thumb to his mouth, and bit. Cameron and Pepe let him spin his wheels and a brief moment later, Taufiq lifted his head. His eyes shifted between the two mock Arabs in front of him. "Who are you two? Why do you want Abbo so bad?"

Pepe stepped closer to Taufiq, "Let's say Abbo took something that does not belong to him."

"And it doesn't really matter if I want to tell you, does it?"

"Not really," said Cameron.

CHAPTER 28
SEVENS RUGBY STADIUM, DUBAI

Taufiq's forehead had gained an oily sheen. His attempt to maintain a confident air was compromised by his feeble and distant words. "You're not going to shoot me?"

"We are not going to shoot you," said Pepe. "Though you can make this easy or hard on yourself."

"Yes, I understand clearly. I will tell you, but it will make no difference. You will never be able to get to him."

"Try us," said Cameron."

"He is at the Burj Khalifa," said Taufiq. "You know this place, the world's tallest building."

"Of course we do," said Pepe. "Can you be more specific?"

"He has a luxury residence in the Armani Hotel, a huge villa suite there. Like a palace really, up in the air, he is safe like a bird in the sky."

"You are sure that is where he is?" asked Pepe. "That does not sound very secure. The Armani is on the lower levels."

"And relatively public," said Cameron. "Like our friend in London."

"But you see," said Taufiq, "he is not in the Armani

residences that everyone knows of. He is high like a falcon on the 105th floor. The residences between floor 77 and 110 are very secure. You must be friend or family to access those levels."

"Or have a key," said Cameron.

The Saudi peered at Cameron.

"Do you have a key?" asked Pepe.

"He has a key," said Cameron. "He has a very special key. Don't you?"

"Taufiq," said Pepe. "Let me see your key."

"It will not help you," said Taufiq.

"Probably not. Let me see anyway."

The Saudi reached his hand into his thobe, removed a golden keycard, and then handed the card to Pepe.

"Hmm," said Pepe. "There is an electronic chip in here, and the card is engraved. Do you mind if my friend takes a look?" Pepe held the card out for Cameron to inspect. Taufiq stared at the ground.

"Well I'll be, that is nice," said Cameron. He held the card up in the air, "A little holographic paint, a chip, engraving. Let's see what this says." He pulled the card closer, "It says here...wow, you live there. That must be nice."

The Saudi, his head still drooping and eyes beginning to well, spoke quietly in almost a murmur, "It is a family residence."

"I bet you have to use a code with this too," said Cameron. "A pin number, maybe?" Cameron peered over the card to Taufiq.

Taufiq began to weep.

"Is that true, Taufiq?" asked Pepe. "Do we need a code?"

Taufiq subtly nodded his head.

"What is the code, Taufiq? Tell us the code. We need your help."

The Saudi spoke in a whisper.

"I am sorry," said Pepe. "I did not hear you."

"823," said the Saudi. "The code is 823. The card works for the elevator and the residence door on the 102nd floor."

"That's what the card says," said Cameron, "102nd floor."

"You see," said Pepe. "That was not so bad. Now we can be close to Abbo. The task is almost complete."

The Saudi nodded again, tears streaming from his eyes.

"And the new woman?" asked Pepe. "The one with chestnut hair and green eyes that has been brought into the harem."

"Also at the Armani Hotel. He keeps his harem there."

"On the same floor?"

"No, one floor below." The Saudi lifted his head, "That key will get you to those floors as well. Except…"

"Except what, Taufiq?" asked Pepe. "Except what?"

"I will need to be with you. Sometimes, not always, sometimes the elevator requests more security."

"Another code?" asked Pepe.

"Or something biometric?" asked Cameron. "Like a voice imprint, a handprint, maybe even a retinal scan."

The Saudi hesitated, then said, "A retinal scan," he paused to gauge Pepe's reaction and then began to speak quickly. "Particularly if you are visiting floors other than your own, it is all very random, hardly ever actually, that's why I didn't think of it, but I will help you, I swear."

"I see," said Pepe.

The Saudi watched Cameron press a thumb to his forehead and make a deep frown.

"I will help you," said the Saudi. "To get Abbo, I will help. Tonight, now. We will go right now."

"That will not be necessary," said Pepe. "You have helped enough. We are finished here."

"Are you sure? There must be more I can do."

"No, you have done enough."

"I have?"

"Now, Taufiq, you must understand we need to be

confident that you will stay silent. If you were to go to Abbo, or run into Abbo, or if Abbo were to come looking for you, there is too great a chance you may say something."

Again the orbs of Taufiq's eyes, plump and pushing from his skull, fought to escape him, "I swear I will say nothing. By Allah I swear, by Allah I swear. Wallah, Wallah."

Pepe placed his hand on the Saudi's shoulder, "I believe, you believe that."

"You promised not to shoot me!" said Taufiq, his face was wet and dripped with tears.

"Shhh," said Pepe. He leaned in close and placed his cheek near Taufiq's. "Shhh."

Taufiq felt a poke in his neck and then great warmth. Pepe pressed on Taufiq's shoulder, easing him slowly down the wall to his knees. Taufiq placed his hand on his neck where he felt the warmth. His fingers immediately became hot and wet and when he massaged them into his neck, sticky. He pulled them away to see his own bright crimson leakage and attempted to cry out, but no sounds came.

"Shhh," said Pepe again. Pepe's face was warm and kind, "Allah waits for you. Close your eyes and go to him."

CHAPTER 29
OLD TOWN DUBAI

Alastair sat at a table near the edge of the promenade overlooking the Burj Khalifa Lake, the building of the shared name towering above them from across the water.

"You didn't bring him with you," said Alastair.

"In a sense, we did," said Cameron. He pulled a chair away from the table and then sat down. "Pepe has his eyes."

"Bloody hell. So it came to that." Alastair's lips pulled tight and the entirety of his face shifted to the side, a scowl that Cameron recognized and always took as a judgment, and a faux disgust. Cameron had adopted many cues from Alastair over the years. Alastair had an upscale upbringing and recognized when to behave in a fashion.

"It always comes to that," said Cameron. "That's why I got the hell out of the game."

A waiter approached Cameron and bowed his head, "Coffee, Sayyed?"

"Yes, coffee please, with lemon and sweet. Do you have artificial?"

"Certainly," said the waiter.

"That will be all then, thank you."

The waiter bowed his head again and backed away from the table before changing direction for the bar.

Alastair picked up where they were a moment before. "You got out of the game for the same reason as the rest of us. You were getting too old and too poor to be doing what we were doing."

"I was tired of killing innocents."

"Collateral happens and you know that. Besides, I would hardly consider Taufiq Sawar an innocent. The man may have lost his money gambling but he made it as a human trafficker, a slave trader. He will not be missed."

Cameron grunted, "Vive la Légion."

"Need I remind you that in combat you act without passion or hatred," said Alastair.

"You are not the only one that can quote the code of honor," said Cameron. "Respect vanquished enemies, I remember that part, too."

"I do as well," said Alastair. "Collateral, we'll have a drink for the bastard later. Does that suit you?"

Cameron flashed a glance and a twisted half smile smirk across the table to Alastair for bringing him back to reality.

"So everything was as we thought?" asked Alastair.

Cameron lifted his hands above the table, "Once again our friend in London had the information right to the tee. The secret Armani residence on the 105th floor of the Burj Khalifa, the golden keycard security, the elevator retinal scanner, and he was even right, unfortunately, that Taufiq would try to double cross us."

"And Christine?"

Cameron sucked in a deep breath, "Right, Christine. He said he saw her, or rather, a new girl with chestnut hair and green eyes that had recently been brought into the harem."

"Harem?"

"Yeah."

The waiter returned to the table and set Cameron's

coffee before him. To the side he set a plate of assorted sugar cubes and sachets of artificial sweeteners. "Shukran," said Cameron.

The waiter bowed his head said, "Afwan," in response and then again backed away from the table.

Alastair watched the waiter from the corner of his eye until he felt he was clear, "Please tell me this harem is on the same floor."

"Close, a floor below," said Cameron. He picked up three yellow sachets from the plate, tore the ends at once together, and spilled the contents into his coffee. He shifted his eyes up toward the tower across the lake, "You come up with any new ideas as to how to get in and out of there while we were gone, or did you spend the whole of the morning with the blonde you disappeared with last night?"

"No and yes, no new ideas and yes I spent a good part of the morning with the blonde. She could not get enough of me."

"I cannot believe you are still using that same line," scoffed Cameron. "'I'm from Kenya.'"

"Well, I am, and the ladies love it."

Cameron twisted and tossed the sliver of lemon rind from the side of his saucer into his cup and then gave a quick stir with the demitasse spoon.

Alastair watched Cameron's ritual and when he was finished, he asked, "Why the artificial sweet?"

"Are you serious?"

"Well, yeah. That raw sugar is good sugar, besides, you're a chef."

"I'm a chef. I eat too much sugar. I am trying to watch my intake."

"Hmm," said Alastair.

"What? I'm getting older. You should watch your diet as well."

"My bloody diet is fine, thank you." Alastair gazed out across the lake. At that moment, the Dubai Fountain, the massive choreographed water system that spread across the manmade Burj Khalifa Lake, erupted and projected water into the air at different heights along the intricate path of the piping.

"Would you look at that," said Cameron.

"Beautiful," said Alastair. The high-pressure water jets and shooters of the fountain pushed streams of water to and fro across each other while the water robots made other streams spin and twirl in such a way that they appeared to dance. "You know that fountain can spray 83,000 liters of water in the air at any moment."

"You don't say," said Cameron, and then sipped from his coffee. He was well aware of where this was about to go.

"I read they installed more than 6,600 lights and twenty-five color projectors."

"Uh huh."

"They even had fire shooting out one year."

"Did they?"

"Can you imagine if that was your job, to be the fountain man?"

"Here we go."

"I mean, what a responsibility to be the man that runs the fountain. What a specialized job. All of that pristine knowledge for only a handful of fountains."

"I've told you before," said Cameron. "These fountains are run by firms, teams, computers."

"But there is one man, Kincaid. One man for each fountain that knows that fountain, that keeps the whole thing running like clockwork. A handful of master fountain men around the world. Sure, the Dubai Fountain is the largest, but think, there is another guy that runs the Bellagio Fountains—"

"Yeah, that reminds me, I read an article in the Times that the same people that built the Bellagio Fountains built the Dubai Fountain, they build all of these fountains."

"That's what I'm saying," said Alastair, "the Fountain of Wealth in Singapore, the Magic Fountain of Montjuic.

Kincaid, the Big Wild Goose Pagoda Fountains were built in 652."

"652, I know, you've told us a hundred times, your fountain fetish is well known and noted, and what I meant was that a firm built these things to be run by firms. I don't think there is just one fountain guy."

"Sure there is."

"I thought we were out here to check out the tower. I should have known."

"Well, I said I have no new ideas, I do have an old one. Watch this," said Alastair. On cue, five super shooters projected streams far above the rest of the water dance. "Whoa, now that is pretty high, at least seventy-five meters."

Cameron followed the jets of water up above the lake. As the water crested, a series of loud booms echoed through Old Town.

"What was that?" asked Cameron.

"The water shooters have to use a lot of pressure to push the water that high. They are very loud. They have extreme shooters they never use that push the water up over a hundred fifty meters. Bloody shame." Alastair winked at Cameron. "They would make your ears rattle."

Cameron slapped his hand down on the table. "Alastair, you are brilliant."

"True," said Alastair. "I have been waiting for chance to be the Fountain Man, at least for a night."

CHAPTER 30
AT.MOSPHERE RESTAURANT, BURJ KHALIFA LEVEL 122, DUBAI

The doors of the express elevator opened on the level 123 sky lobby, 450 meters above the promenade of the Dubai mall, where Cameron and Alastair shared coffee earlier in the day.

"Now this is class," said Cameron, the movement of his lips imperceptible as he spoke. No longer dressed in the incognito local garb of the thobe and ghutra, he nonchalantly adjusted the cuffs of his collar shirt and the Armani dinner jacket he'd purchased from the boutique, "Can you fellas hear me all right?"

From a small device hidden on the inside of Cameron's ear, Pepe responded, "You are coming in clear."

"Crystal," said Alastair. "Can you hear us?"

"Perfectly," said Cameron. From the express elevator, Cameron entered onto the top of a two-story art installation of dynamic light and ambient music. "You wouldn't believe this place."

"I am sure," said Pepe, "though I do not think just anyone can land a same-day reservation for the At.mosphere restaurant, Monsieur Dragon Chef."

"Very true, that's not what I meant, though," said Cameron

"I thought that girl at reception was going to faint," said Alastair.

"Very funny, you two should put on a show. Listen, out of the elevator there is an amazing mahogany cantilevered staircase that is lit up as elaborately as that fountain show down in the lake. Which, by the way, I can see clearly out of the floor to ceiling window 123 floors below, along with everything else in Dubai."

"Cantilevered staircase. You mean suspended in mid-air?" asked Alastair.

"Exactly, I'm telling you, this is surreal. Remember those computer flight simulations we used to sit through? Well oddly, they were more realistic than this. I swear there is a toy city to my left."

"You're high enough up for a low flight plan," said Alastair. "What is to your right?"

"And to my right, below me, is the entrance to the restaurant, mahogany walls, the floors are café au lait limestone and hand tufted carpets, and I am pretty sure the furnishings are Adam Tihany."

"Adam who?" asked Alastair.

"Adam Tihany," said Pepe. "He designs all of the restaurants and hotels. Kincaid goes on about him sometimes."

"Adam Tihany is widely regarded as the preeminent hospitality designer in the world today," said Cameron.

"See," said Pepe.

"Gotcha," said Alastair. "I don't suppose you see the target."

"No, not yet. Give me a moment, here comes Peter, the maître d'. I usually try not to be too obvious."
Cameron lifted his arms and raised his voice, "Peter, good to see you."

Peter, a tall thin Brit, glided toward the landing of the

stairs, his hands clasped and raised to Cameron, still a few steps up. "Cameron Kincaid, welcome, welcome, so great to see you. I could not have been more pleased when you called." Peter placed both of his hands around Cameron's and Cameron in turn lifted his arm to Peter's shoulder. The two walked together side by side.

"What brings you to Dubai?" asked Peter. "Opening a little competition, perhaps?"

"Not on this trip, though I could hardly compete with what you have here. You said if I were ever in the neighborhood to stop by, so..."

"Certainly we are so glad to have you, and thank you so much for the compliment, I so enjoyed Le Dragon Vert. Your restaurant is a true jewel in New York. We have worked hard with what we have. You have to see what the chef has done with the Josper oven."

"I intend to," said Cameron, "literally cooking without gas."

The two entered the lounge area. The dramatic ambience of the suspended stairwell was accentuated with heavy hues of amethyst and a complex blending of ornate velvets. Cameron realized now that the esoteric music he had heard since coming off the express elevator originated from the harpist playing near the end of the bar. Peter led Cameron toward a small table. Cameron veered to the high bar, the sheer white backlit glass reminiscent of the milk bars of the last century.

"I'm fine at the bar, Peter," said Cameron. He rattled his fingertips across the edge of the bar and spun back toward Peter. "Even from here the view is incredible."

Peter shifted his view to the same direction. "Yes, we have a spectacular view of World and Palm Islands from here and of course, Atlantis at the end. And over there..."

"The Burj al Arab. Yes, I see."

Peter smiled and nodded.

Pepe and Alastair had been anticipating Cameron's statement, 'Even from here the view is incredible,' as that meant he had sighted their target, Abbo Mohammed. Now would Abbo see Cameron? The plan was simple. They knew Abbo regularly dined in the At.mosphere Lounge and they knew that Abbo was by nature a connoisseur of cuisine, celebrity, and of all things deemed great and fine. Cameron had dropped his cover to secure a reservation at the At.mosphere, anticipating an encounter with Abbo. Cameron's plan was to have the maître d' place him at the bar near Abbo and let natural events play out. The team had calculated that Abbo, once noticing Cameron, would be excited at an opportunity to meet the celebrity Dragon Chef, and would insist Cameron join him at his table. Abbo, of course, would have no idea that Cameron Kincaid, the famous New York celebrity chef, was one of the numbers involved in his son's disappearance.

"Would you mind indulging me for a closer look?" asked Cameron.

"Certainly," said Peter. He nodded to the bartender, "Edward can you prepare a —" he glanced at Cameron.

"A lemon seltzer would be fine," said Cameron.

Peter again nodded with a closed smile and then led Cameron toward the seaward window, a path that ran directly next to Abbo's table. Abbo sat at the small table's head between two elegantly dressed chestnut haired women. Cameron crossed directly in front of Abbo. He did not make eye contact, yet he revealed as much of his face as he could to be sure Abbo had a good look, at one point pausing to glance across the room. Abbo was not an unhandsome man. Dressed debonair, his dark Somali complexion seemed almost regal in the complimentary interior of the At.mosphere Lounge. The contours of his strong cheeks and jaw were reminiscent of his son Feizel. The women beside Abbo almost caused Cameron to stall in his stride, each a visage of Christine.

Resolute, Cameron pressed forward to the window, "Breathtaking, Peter, absolutely breathtaking. What can't you see?" Another code for Pepe and Alastair, meaning

Christine was not with Abbo.

"We are very fortunate." Peter leaned in to Cameron, "Though this is not New York."

"Beautiful all the same," said Cameron.

The two sauntered back toward the bar. Abbo was speaking rapidly to the woman to his left and she in turn was relating what he said to her mirror on his other side. All three were flashing glances in Cameron's direction as he drew closer. When Cameron and Peter were about to reach the end of Abbo's table, he spoke, his voice deep, booming, "Excuse me, Sayyed, a thousand pardons. My lady friend insists that you are the television chef Cameron Kincaid."

Abbo had taken the bait.

Cameron stopped at the end of the table and smiled a wide, toothy unassuming smile, the smile he reserved for television and fans.

"Yes, sir, I am," said Cameron.

Peter placed his hand on Cameron's shoulder, "Mister Cameron Kincaid, may I introduce Mister Abbo Mohammed."

CHAPTER 31
AT.MOSPHERE RESTAURANT, BURJ KHALIFA LEVEL 122, DUBAI

Many aspects of Abbo Mohammed were fitting for such a man of his physical stature while others were magnified by pure narcissism. Every gesture was flamboyant, surreal, and larger than life. To hear Abbo speak was peculiar; though he had not mastered the English language, his voice was deep, clear, and each word was enunciated at the peril of being missed. His posture was unnaturally erect. His eyes cast a sidelong leer to Cameron across the table, "Mister Kincaid, thank you so much for joining us." Cameron gauged Abbo was a man that sought to peer deeply into the minds of others, to decipher them. "How fortunate for us that you happened by. Can I offer you some champagne?" In a broad flowing display, he extended his arm to present the bottle of Ruinart Rose chilling in a tableside ice bucket.

"I'm afraid I am limited to seltzer and lemon this evening," said Cameron, his voice apologetic, that of the fool to match the toothy grin he still wore. He placed his hand above his stomach, "All of the travelling."

Abbo widely smiled in return, tilted his head slightly to the side, and then nodded. "I understand quite well. My last trip to New York threw me for many days. All of the long flying, I believe."

Through Cameron's hidden microphone, Pepe and Alastair were able to hear Abbo's deep voice stumbling through English with defiant clarity. As according to plan, Abbo had recognized Cameron and invited him to his table. All Cameron's team needed to do was wait for the next phase.

"I am sorry, I have been rude," said Abbo. "May I introduce Mary and Antoinette?" The beautiful dark haired women, one on each arm, wore silk camisoles in lieu of blouses, one patterned with red roses and trimmed with Habutai lace, the other less conservative in comparison, a sequined sheer black silk tank top.

"Hello," said Cameron. He shifted his eyes to each of the women, "Marie and Toinette."

"Mary," said red roses. "And Antoinette," corrected sequined sheer.

"Ah."

"Hello. Welcome to Dubai," said Mary, her voice that of a trade show hostess.

Cameron's eyes widened.

"You are surprised by my American accent, Mister Kincaid?"

"Should I be?"

Mary coyly lowered her green eyes away from Cameron to a solitary sugar cube plated before her. She playfully twirled the cube around the saucer with the end of her red enameled fingernail, "Some men are."

"I am not some men."

Mary flirtatiously tilted her head and eased a glance up at Cameron, "I am sure you are not."

"Yes," laughed Abbo. "Mary is from middle of America."

"I am from Belgium," said Antoinette, her green eyes

puppy wide, her long enameled nail pressing the edge of her lower lip.

"So then it is true," said Cameron.

"What is, Mister Kincaid?" asked Antoinette.

"Dubai is the land of many delights."

Abbo laughed deeply.

"That amuses you?" asked Cameron.

Abbo composed himself, "You are a man that appreciates fine things. Please be my guest and educate me in the designs of this menu," he paused and shifted his pupils side to side to each of the women. "And dessert is on me. What do you say?"

Cameron maintained an aloof tone, "I say let's order the first course."

CHAPTER 32
PARIS COUNTRYSIDE, FIFTEEN YEARS BEFORE

Christine peered over the crinkled road atlas into the withered brown field. "The farm is supposed to be right up here," she said. "That is an orchard."

"Where there is an orchard there is usually a farm house," said Cameron. "I'm sure the farmhouse is right over this rise." He wrapped his fingers tightly around the knob of the gear stick and lunged his shoulder forward. The gearbox of the old Citroen 2CV ratcheted loudly, resisting his effort. He nudged the shifter again. The car jolted forward, then the motor began purring smoothly up the hill.

"There, you see?" said Cameron.

Through the tops of the bare scraggly orchard trees, the crest of the hill revealed the weathered tin and shingle roof of a barn. Christine held the atlas tightly to her chest, straightened her back, and then extended her neck. The corners of her cheeks rose and she spoke with an elevated pitch, inhaling her words, "Oui, oui, that is the farm, Cameron."

As the Citroen topped the hill, the rest of the farm was

revealed. The house was attached to the barn. The aged stonework façade was intermingled across the two buildings. Christine began to tap her feet. By the time the car reached the small bridge at the bottom of the hill, she had started to slap Cameron's thigh to punctuate her remarks, "Look, look! See those little chocolate pooches in the yard. How cute!"

Cameron wheeled the Citroen into the pebbled drive of the farm and began the fight with the gear stick to shift the car into neutral. Christine did not wait for him to turn off the ignition. As soon as the vehicle slowed, she opened the thin door and made her way to the band of puppies frolicking in the yard. The gearbox quarreled loudly, yet above that were Christine's giggles and laughs.

Having successfully parked the car, Cameron opened his door and spun his feet out onto the stony driveway. He stayed seated for a moment, captured by the splendor of Christine rolling on the lawn with four puppies on top of her. Little chocolate labs near the same color as her long, now wild and sprawling, chestnut hair. Whimsically, she snickered and smirked. She communed with the small animals with quirky squeals and squeaks. Christine allowed the little paws of one to push her to one side and the muzzle of another to toss her onto her back. She let them bathe her face with thousands of little tongue kisses.

Cameron was mesmerized by the amount of joy these Labrador pups brought this innocent beauty. The image became interspersed with lightning flashes of chestnut haired children rolling across the lawn with their mother. Cameron saw himself there in the yard as well. In that instant, Cameron saw a possible future of a family in love and at play.

CHAPTER 33
ABBO'S HAREM SUITE, BURJ KHALIFA
LEVEL 104, DUBAI

Cameron stood at the corner of the glass walled suite, high above the city of Dubai. He peered into the vast blanket of twinkling lights that speckled far out toward the Middle Eastern horizon. Relieved of his Armani dinner jacket, he still wore his collared shirt and slacks. His tie was loose yet knotted. Mary had disrobed for him. He had smiled and then faced the window. Perhaps she thought him coy, playing a game, while ironically he was at odds facing her beauty, a beauty so reminiscent of Christine. Mary stepped up behind Cameron, seductive in her stride, and slowly draped her arms around his shoulders, resting her cheek against his back.

"You made a wise choice," said Mary. She pressed her naked body against Cameron.

"Did I?"

Mary held Cameron as Christine often had, her arms wrapped around his broad chest, her head resting on his shoulders, her pert breasts pushed into his back. Christine was most likely captive in the next room awaiting liberation from Abbo. In facing the window, Christine's memory had been invoked rather than defused. Cameron had a mission that Mary was part of, yet an act so natural as being with a woman, a woman devoted to indulging sensual pleasures, was at the moment the cause of mental duress.

"You know, Abbo is rarely so generous," said Mary, her nimble fingers worked the knot of Cameron's necktie, effortlessly loosening the silken material.

"Is that so?" He raised the end of the now loose tie and slowly pulled the thin piece of silk from around his neck.

"Well, he only shares me with very special men." Mary unfastened the second and third buttons of Cameron's shirt and then slid her hand beneath the tight fabric to slowly caress his flesh.

"He considers me special?" asked Cameron. He felt her sigh deeply behind him, quivering as her widespread fingers tightly strummed along his muscular chest. Cameron rested the lids of his eyes closed and allowed himself to release his restriction. In his lowered hands, he folded the long tie mid-length, then slid his hands to either end.

Cameron remained still, flexing his chest with deep breathes that further excited Mary and prompted her to eagerly unfasten the other buttons of his shirt, until his naked front was a field of flesh for her wide spread hands to soak in all at once.

Since Abbo had invited Cameron to 'try' Mary, Pepe and Alastair had maintained silence, all the while listening through his hidden mike. When Alastair spoke into his ear, he was not surprised. "You are special, Kincaid," said Alastair, mirroring Mary's sensuous tone. The levity was reminiscent to past undercover missions when Alastair would observe from a distance rooftop or darkened window. "Any sign of Christine?"

Cameron was not in a position to respond. With the silk tie firmly in his grasp, he slid his fingers over Mary's and entangled her hands into his.

"Of all those green eyed girls, you stood out," said Cameron.

Mary cooed, then said, "The sheikh like girls with chestnut hair and green eyes."

There was no visual component to the surveillance kit, only the earpiece and the microphone. Alastair and Pepe were not privy to what Cameron had seen. They did not see Mary and Antoinette at the table eighteen floors above, nor did they see the other women lounging half naked in the communal area of the harem suite. Abbo Mohammed had a deep fetish for women of a certain type and had built up a collection. Cameron painted a picture with the clues he dropped in conversing with Mary, so that they could understand.

"Oh my," said Alastair. "That is wrong."

"Cameron," said Pepe, "find her and get her out of there."

Cameron released one of Mary's hands to ease her around to the front of him in a way that allowed the tie to encircle her and then, his head bowed, he pulled the strip of silk to bring her against him, so that they pressed cheek to cheek. The heat of her breath burned into him. He slid his lips across her face and into her mouth.

Cameron kissed Mary deeply and she tasted sweet. His kiss excited her. She pressed herself into him, to devour him. She clutched the sides of his shirt and pulled. He tightened the hold of the tie around her upper shoulders to stay her arms. She fell to her knees and frantically positioned herself to take him into her mouth.

"Hold on," said Cameron. "Not too fast. Let me help you to the bed."

With a smile, Mary gazed up at Cameron and then rested herself into the slack of the tie. "You're the boss," she said. The tie became Mary's reins and Cameron held the ends tightly. Playfully, she maneuvered herself over to the bed. Cameron let loose the tie as she climbed onto the mattress.

Mary rose to her knees to where Cameron stood at the end of the bed.

"So how does an American girl end up in Dubai?" asked Cameron.

"I knew that enticed you." Mary clutched the sides of Cameron's open shirt again. She opened her mouth wide to fully kiss him, pushed her tongue against his chest, and then slowly raked her teeth closed, once, then twice, and then tilted her head up. "I was doing an escort trip with an older man, an American, to Kuwait city and one of Abbo's men discovered me."

"Discovered you? You were abducted?"

"No, silly, though that's kinky. I was offered a two year contract for more money than I ever thought I would see, and that was three years ago."

"A contract?"

"Sure, all of the girls here are under two year contracts. I am the exception. Not bad for a girl from Iowa."

"No, I suppose not."

Mary nuzzled against Cameron again, "I would do you for free though, even if Abbo had not asked. I have to admit I'm a bit of a celebrity groupie. A celebophile."

Alastair spoke in Cameron's earpiece, "I think I'm becoming ill."

"So nobody is here against their will?" asked Cameron.

Mary rested down on her shins and peered deep into Cameron. "Not at all," she lifted the silk tie from the mattress. "But, I suppose if you like your concubines tied," she wound the silk around her wrists and then raised them to Cameron, "we can play that game."

"That's not what I meant. Someone said something to me about the new girl."

"I assure you that little French whore got a great contract. She used to be a model, I think."

"Now, Cameron," said Pepe.

"Where is she, the new girl?"

"Why do you care? You have me."

Cameron lifted Mary close to deliver a passionate kiss. He inhaled as he kissed her, taking the air from her, causing her to swoon. He eased back. A faint plea of a breath slipped from her, his charm overwhelming. He lowered his voice, "I was thinking maybe..."

Mary was anxious, "Oh, you are greedy." She bit her lower lip and then said, "I'd rather have you to myself, but that could be fun. I have wanted to try her out since she came in. C'mon, let's go get her."

Mary spryly launched herself from the mattress, towing Cameron by his shirt.

"You know I interviewed her," Mary teased.

"What does that mean?"

Mary, comfortably nude in the dim light of the suite, glanced back at Cameron with a coy smile, "Wouldn't you love to know."

The hallway from the master bedroom led toward the center of the suite that sprawled almost the entirety of the floor. Mary walking naked through the corridor had no affect on the other tenants, all of whom were in different stages of dress, most topless in only panties, others fully nude.

"To interview means I look for what the sheikh likes and make sure flaws do not slip through. I have been with him the longest and know quite well what demeanor fits best."

They crossed the lounge area of the suite and entered the hallway leading into the other wing.

"So you actually interview?"

"In all kinds of places, all around the world. This is her room here." Mary knocked lightly on the closed door, "Babette, it's me Mary. I have a handsome present for you."

"Babette?" asked Cameron.

"Yes, I told you she is French, from Marseille I believe."

The door opened to a beautiful green-eyed girl.

Daniel Arthur Smith

"It's not her," said Cameron.

"Excuse me?" said Babette.

Cameron spun around and pushed open the door across the hall, startling a girl painting her toenails on her bed. "What are you doing?" asked Mary. Cameron continued down the hall, opening one door, and then the next, "She's not here. She must be upstairs."

"Understood," said Pepe. "I am on my way."

CHAPTER 34
BURJ KHALIFA LEVEL 104, DUBAI

Cameron backed into the corridor, holding the door of Abbo Mohammed's 104th floor harem suite slightly open with the toe of his shoe. He slipped on his Armani dinner jacket, extended his arms, and then flexed his neck side to side. From the inside of his jacket, he retrieved two smooth stainless steel cylinders, the size and shape of cigar flasks. He twisted the metal dials affixed to the ends of the tubes to wind each counter clockwise and then held them up to ensure they were slowly spinning clockwise again. Cameron tossed each, one at a time, with a swift underhand pitch, back into the heart of the suite. From the door, the far glass wall lent a vastness to the space.

"These are going to be enough to gas the whole flat?" he asked.

From the tiny device resting inside of his ear canal, Alastair replied, "The compression on those canisters will disburse the gas across the entire floor. If you sent two cans into the central area, they're going to waft in an amnesia fog."

Pepe added, "In a few moments, they will never remember that celebrity chef Cameron Kincaid paid them a visit."

"Hmm," said Cameron. "Their loss." He smirked, and then gently eased the door closed with his cuff.

That part of the mission finished, Cameron snapped his fingers on both hands then reached up to fasten the knot of his tie, spinning on his outward foot toward the elevator.

In the center of the corridor, a muscular man in a dark suit was peering at Cameron. Cameron smiled at the man and sauntered past him to the front of the elevator, the whole while adjusting the knot of his tie.

"Excuse me, sir," said the man, now behind Cameron's shoulder.

"Yes?" said Cameron. He focused on his dull reflection in the stainless steel doors, and then quaffed his hair with the palm of his hand.

"What did you throw into that suite?"

"I'm sorry?" Cameron ran his index finger over his brows, indifferent to the man's inquiry.

"You threw something back into the suite when you stepped out. What was it?"

"Oh," Cameron gestured his thumb back to the door, "you mean when I…?"

"Yes, when you exited the door."

"Well, those were gas canisters. Like knockout gas, except those were for forgetting, kind of roofied them all at once, if you will."

The man drew a handgun from the inside of his jacket and directed the business end into Cameron's back. "Sir, you better step away from the elevator."

"Okay," said Cameron. He slipped one foot far to his side and then slowly began to drag his other foot to meet the first. The gunman's muzzle followed Cameron. Above them, the digital floor indicator dinged and the doors to the elevator began to slide open. The doors were divided no wider than a fist when the sound of two mosquitos whizzed past Cameron into the forehead of the gunman. Two men in technical service jumpsuits emblazoned with the swirling logo of the Dubai Fountain stood in the elevator. Each of the men wore a heavy utility belt, had a balaclava mask drawn down over his face, and held an MP-5 submachine gun in hand.

Cameron entered between the two and then spun around to face to opening.

"We done here?" asked Pepe.

"Yep," said Cameron.

Pepe and Alastair let go of the doors.

"You seem back in the game," said Pepe. From a duffel bag at his side, he removed another MP-5 and balaclava facemask for Cameron.

"Reluctantly," said Cameron, rapidly inspecting the weapon.

Alastair slid the keycard the Saudi had given them into the elevator console. "I never left," said Alastair. He tapped the numbers one, zero, and five and then punched the code, eight, two, and three.

"Going up," said Alastair.

The elevator floated to the next level in an instant. The interior console dinged with the same tone that the digital floor indicator had resonated in the corridor below. This time the doors did not separate. A thin crimson LED rectangle lit up high up on the console panel in front of Alastair's face. Within the rectangle glowed a crimson LED circle.

"I figure thirty seconds before downstairs looks in on us," said Cameron. He fit the facemask over his head.

"I wouldn't worry about the cameras. I was able to rig the elevator on a loop," said Alastair. He eased his head to the side to inspect the ocular scan from a different angle and then reached out his hand in front of Cameron. Pepe unsnapped the leather cover of one of the front utility belt pockets. From within he retrieved a hard sunglass case, a Ray Ban logo imprinted across the top.

Alastair saw the case in a side glance and then shifted his head around, "Oh, you didn't. I was looking for that.

That's my sunglass case."

"I had to put them in something safe," said Pepe. He flipped open the case to reveal a plastic baggy filled with ice and the two plump eyes of Taufiq Sawar. "This is a good case, strong."

"Just hand the thing over," said Alastair.

Cameron sucked in his chest as Pepe passed the cadaver specimen across the elevator. He curled his lip. He was not disturbed the two gruesome jelly orbs peering up from the case. Rather, he was displeased with Taufiq's fate.

"It was necessary," said Pepe. "You see that now."

Cameron cleared his throat and rolled his eyes to Pepe. "I knew that then. I don't have to like the situation."

Pepe was undeterred by his friend's suggestion of empathy. "Did I hear you correct that all of the women in Abbo's harem look like Christine?"

"This should do fine," said Alastair. He held the case up to the ocular scanner. The backlit LED circle and rectangle flicked from crimson to emerald.

"Yeah," said Cameron, "he has a fetish for caucasian women with green eyes and chestnut hair."

"Then I have no problem with the situation," said Pepe. "Get ready."

The elevator doors separated.

Outside of the elevator were two suit dressed security men, each with a hole in his forehead before he could draw his own weapon. With a mechanical rhythm stemmed from engrained training, Alastair stowed Taufiq's eyes, secured his duffel, and then entered the corridor. Alastair's comrades followed in fluent motion, Cameron holding left, and then Pepe squatted to drag his duffel out between the two dropped men. Pepe methodically sifted through the clothes of the corpses for radios and access cards. Alastair merely reached back to receive the coming bounty, his gaze fixed on the door of the 105th floor master suite.

Pepe finished rifling through the suited dead, set a charge beneath the sleeve of one, and then the three men edged toward Abbo's door.

It occurred suddenly to Cameron that after years of focusing on building a reputation as a restaurateur, he was now executing his second direct action infiltration and exfiltration in a week.

The three stopped at the door, each in position to charge and indiscriminately fire. Alastair pressed the muzzle of his MP-5 firmly against the surface of the door. He placed three fingers on the steel latch and between his index finger and thumb held the access card to the mouth of the slot. Calmly he asked, "Ready?"

The responses were as cool. "Clear," said Pepe.

"Clear," said Cameron.

Alastair slid the access card into the slot below the latch. The crimson LED on the top of the access reader blinked off and the neighboring LED lit bright emerald.

"Vive la Légion," said Alastair as he pressed down on the latch with his other three fingers and forced the door open with the muzzle of his MP-5.

CHAPTER 35
ABBO'S SUITE, BURJ KHALIFA LEVEL 105, DUBAI

The guard assigned to monitor the closed circuit video of the corridor outside of Abbo's 105th floor suite had his back to the door and his feet up on the small table that made up his makeshift security desk. Rather than watching the small screen in front of him, he was flipping through a comic book. He did not so much as flinch when Alastair forced the door with his MP-5. Too many years babysitting the secure suite had made the man complacent. Perhaps the guard thought one of the men from the corridor was coming in to use the restroom, or perhaps he did not hear the door as he was so wrapped up in the colored pictures of his magazine. Whatever the reason the guard did not bother to react did not matter. Alastair, Pepe, and Cameron would never find out. Before the door swung wide, the cheap pressed paper of the comic book was soaked with blood and brains.

In a mindful instant, the three men surveyed the hallway before them. The commandos had studied the floor layout from an acquired set of blueprints. Abbo's suite was supposed to mirror the harem suite a floor below and so far the entrance appeared as expected. They had entered into a hallway that opened to a larger central room. Along the hall were two doors. They expected one to be the bathroom and the other, they had decided, was a room for the guards. Cameron flipped off the power switch for the light. The other switches were at the far end of the hallway, past the doors, before the central room. Even Pepe, forced to wear glasses to read, was at home in the dark. The three edged forward. Light music rose from another far off room in the suite, as well as deep bellowing laughter, the unmistakable laughter of Abbo Mohammed. Cameron slipped into the first side door, a darkened bathroom, and then, confident no one was hiding inside, eased back behind Alastair. Pepe ducked into the room on his side of the hall and then returned with a nod designating that space also clear.

Each planted small charges along their path.

The three stopped at the end of the hallway. Mere meters away from where they stood, the edge of the suite met the Dubai night. The Middle Eastern horizon beyond was crystal clear from this height.

Cameron had already been through the harem suite below. Level 104 had not been modified from the layout they had read. Since the entrance hall and the two side rooms matched the plans, Cameron was confident that Abbo's suite would be similarly unchanged. From the blueprints, they learned that a central room encompassed a large area of the suite. To the left would be the kitchen, dining room, and a few small bedrooms, similar to where Mary led him to Babette in the floor below. Wrapping to the right would be another small bedroom, and then Abbo's master bedroom. The Burj Khalifa tower utilities and other elevators made up the rest of the floor on the opposite side of the corridor.

The number of guards in the suite was an unknown factor and a major risk. Striking the lights in the central room could signal additional guards and unwanted issue.

There had been no immediate response to the clack of Alastair's spent MP-5, loud even with the attached suppressor. That was a good sign, yet the burnt odor already filled the confines of the hallway and would shortly be spreading through the suite, demanding attention.

The bellow of Abbo's laughter echoed again. The warlord's laughter paired with images of Christine shot a pang through Cameron he did not recognize. He wanted to charge the master bedroom regardless of the plan.

A greater will seized him.

The tactician within Cameron introduced a scenario.

Cameron had deduced the warlord must be in the master bedroom, in the bedroom with Christine. That was the direction Abbo's laughter was coming from. Cameron had been in the master bedroom below with Mary. The room Abbo used on his visits to the harem. Cameron figured an easy gamble, for Abbo's own comfort, the harem suite and this floor, would share roughly the same decor. He tapped Alastair's shoulder and then eased himself as forward as he could without entering the central room. Directly outward from their position at the end of the hall the glass walls formed a corner. Relying on the reflective surface of the wall, they surveyed the room. From the reflection they could see two large sofas to their right.

Cameron's suspicions were correct.

Cameron calculated there would be at least one guard in that direction. Somebody more important than a guard, somebody Abbo could call on to fetch something. There had been a bodyguard in the restaurant, a dark Somali the size of a titan. Abbo had called the bodyguard Theal. That bodyguard had not gone down to the harem and was not one of those the three had shot upon entering the suite. Cameron tilted his head out a bit further, wary that reflections show two ways.

On one of the sofas, Cameron could see a man reclining, facing out into the night. A large black man with his eyes closed, possibly sleeping. The man was Theal.

Cameron signaled to Alastair. Alastair understood there was a man sleeping around the corner. Cameron also gestured to Pepe that he would march out around toward the kitchen.

The three matched eyes and nods and then flowed from the hallway. The three filed from out in a well-rehearsed formation, three bulldozers clearing the space. Alastair circled around Cameron to cover the right side of the room where the giant slept while Cameron launched from the shadowed hall into the opposite direction. Behind him followed Pepe, scanning from the left and then settling next to Alastair. They found no confrontation. The only guard in the central room was the man on the sofa, and he would never wake again.

Cameron continued to sweep his wing of the suite, the kitchen, dining room, and other bedrooms. All were clear, no guards, no Christine.

Christine was the woman in the master bedroom with Abbo.

Cameron spun back toward that end of the apartment, his MP-5 forward, his steps wide and swift. He recounted the rooms in fleeting checks, deck clear, walls clear, ceiling clear, check, check, and check. Departing gifts for each room, charge engaged with a twist, applied to the inside of the door jam.

Cameron's heartbeat was in his neck, closing his throat. His body and action were truly autonomous. He crossed the central room and pressed down the hallway toward the master bedroom.

Alastair and Pepe waited outside of the slightly open bedroom door, set to pounce.

The hallway was long and the last steps eternal.

From the bedroom Abbo laughed again deeply, sickly, and there was the sound of another, of a woman, breathing in heavy rhythm, fornicating.

Cameron's eyes were locked on Alastair and Pepe. Their heads subtly nodded in a rhythm to his steps, timing his entry, their launch.

The door burst open to let Cameron cross the threshold.

"Don't move!" screamed Alastair as he and the other two commandos stormed the room and surrounded Abbo, naked on the master bed, beneath the woman he was enjoying an instant before.

Abbo's bright white eyes beamed wild, practically lunging out of his skull toward the three invaders. Mounted on Abbo's groin, her back to the three, was a woman, naked and beading in sweat. His large hands firmly clutched the thin waist of the woman, almost encircling her, a Caucasian woman with long flowing chestnut hair.

CHAPTER 36
ABBO'S SUITE, BURJ KHALIFA LEVEL 105, DUBAI

Cameron, Alastair, and Pepe had long ago learned through early on that compartmentalization is the perfect unconscious psychological defense mechanism, used to avoid cognitive dissonance or the mental discomfort and anxiety caused by having conflicting values, cognitions, emotions, or beliefs. Perhaps that is why, when still physically and mentally acute, they mustered out. To scan a room out of the corner of ones eye and then, in less than a second, calculate the next action may appear an inhuman mechanistic ability, yet the judgment to make the instantaneous call, stems from the soldier's humanity.

Humanity was the reason soldiers were not sent on missions that involved them personally.

Soldiers could not be expected to compartmentalize a hostage situation involving their sister; at any point in the operation the risk was too high that soldier could compromise himself, could compromise the mission.

Yet there was no one else for this mission.

Perhaps Pepe had lost his edge.

Perhaps Pepe was merely a super soldier.

Pepe did not utilize his attuned peripheral vision entering Abbo's bedroom. When the door burst wide, he focused on those two bright white beaming eyes and in an instant he was directly over Abbo, the muzzle of his MP-5 thrust into Abbo's forehead.

The window of Pepe's mask revealing his upper face and eyes blazed varying shades of red. On no other mission had his blood burned. The rapidly forming beads of sweat appeared pink across his brow.

The muscles through Pepe's chest and upper body clenched and flexed tight as his arm extended forward, sinking Abbo's skull deep into the pillow. A vein shot up on Pepe's forehead and neck and, though anatomically incorrect, appeared to pierce right down into his hand, into the submachine gun, into Abbo.

Abbo cried out, a blood ring saturated where muzzle cut into flesh.

"Pepe," said Cameron.

Pepe did not respond. He leered at Abbo, into Abbo, he owned Abbo Mohammed.

"Pepe," said Cameron again. "It's not her. She's not Christine."

Pepe blinked heavy, his stare still given to Abbo, first one blink and then another, a wince, and then another.

"This isn't Christine," said Cameron, his voice somber.

Pepe's eyelids blinked heavy again, then again, meaty steaks slapping his eyes to attention, and then slowly he shifted his gaze up across the bed to Cameron and Alastair.

"Quoi?" asked Pepe.

"This is not Christine," said Alastair.

For the first time since entering the room, Pepe, the once super soldier trained to be mindful, to see all at once, looked into the face of the woman mounted naked on Abbo.

The woman was hyperventilating, crying, her cheeks streaming with tears. From far inside her throat, barely audible sighs and squeaks escaped in rapid burst. Her entire body quivered and she was barely able to hold herself up on the man she had been entertaining seconds ago.

"This is Antoinette," said Cameron.

CHAPTER 37
ABBO'S SUITE, BURJ KHALIFA LEVEL 105, DUBAI

Alastair removed the crumpled linen from the foot of the bed to drape the trembling woman's nude body. He tenderly placed his hands on her now covered shoulders and gently removed her from the groin of the titanic warlord. She let Alastair ease her to the floor. Her breathing, already elevated, increased, and her lower lip began to rapidly quiver. The subtle sighs and squeaks that had fought to escape her an instant before became squawks and caws as the woman, really not more than a girl, slipped into hysterics.

"Shhh," said Alastair. He held the girl's shoulders firm and gentle in his hands. "We're not going to hurt you. You're okay." He squatted to her height then matched his calm blue eyes to hers, "Breathe. You're okay. Breathe in through your nose, like this."

As Cameron watched Alastair calm the woman, he thought how different she was now from earlier in the evening, from the playful young woman at the table in the At.mosphere restaurant. The woman in the restaurant floors above had been flirtatious and seductive, but that had been before three armed commandos stormed the master bedroom and mentally overwhelmed her. She was now in shock and as a broken child.

"Out through your mouth," said Alastair, "there."

Her name was Antoinette.

"Again, breathe in through your nose, that's right."

Antoinette and the other girl that had been with Abbo, Mary, each had green eyes and wore their chestnut hair in the same fashion as Christine. That was Abbo's thing, his fetish. All of the women in the warlord's harem could pass for Christine, or sisters she never had.

"Okay, now, can you take a walk with me?" asked Alastair. He began escorting Antoinette out of the master bedroom.

Cameron had seen girls like Antoinette on countless missions. Things were going to get worse in her world before they got better. For the moment, though, she would be okay.

Cameron rolled his eyes back over to Pepe.

Pepe was calm now. The window in his mask was no longer the index shades of Dante's inferno. There had been a time when the stress of the moment would not have edged Pepe. Fortunately, his tactical training kicked in with a slight push from Cameron. Cameron had said his name a number of times before the outside world registered and then Pepe literally blinked himself back to the moment.

The muzzle of Pepe's MP-5 was still pressed against the warlord's head. Not with the same skull crushing force he applied during what Cameron could only define as a rage, yet with still enough pressure to ensure Abbo was not going to flinch.

Yes, that had been pure rage.

Cameron had recognized the fervor in Pepe's eyes. He had seen that same madness many times before on the faces of enemy combatants that fought with a cultish intensity beyond reason. He thought himself and his team above and immune to such irrational emotive drive. Yet this warlord, Abbo Mohammed, had hijacked a yacht with Pepe's sister on board. To liberate Christine, they had stormed the warlord's Somali compound only to discover Abbo had separated her from the other hostages. Christine was to have a role in his Dubai harem.

That was the intel they had.

Christine was their motivation, and each hour she was held hostage would push them closer to the edge. Cameron was not surprised by Pepe's reflex, entering the room to find Christine serving as a concubine to a warlord, to witness her act of forced fornication.

The woman in the master room was not Christine, nor was she engaged in the act of forced fornication.

Christine was not in the suite and she had not been with the harem.

Their self made mission had a primary objective of infiltration and exfiltration of one primary target, Christine Laroque. Now the mission had taken a turn.

CHAPTER 38
ABBO'S SUITE, BURJ KHALIFA LEVEL 105, DUBAI

Abbo Mohammed sat propped against his headboard. A crimson stream trickled from the center of his forehead where the muzzle of Pepe's MP-5 had broken the skin.

"What do you think you are doing?" said Abbo, the baritone of his voice resonating with contempt.

Cameron lifted a pillow from the side of the massive bed, "Here, you can cover yourself up."

"Does my manhood make you feel inferior?" Abbo shot Cameron a judging leer. "Good. I feel no shame. You should have shame. Thieves in the night, and you, Cameron Kincaid, I see you beneath your mask. You think you can steal from me?"

"We aren't here to steal," said Cameron. He dropped the pillow.

"No matter," said Abbo, his voice confident and deep. "You will not leave alive. My men will never let you leave."

Pepe had composed himself. "They are all dead."

"You think the men in other room and the hall are the only soldiers that protect me. You are foolish. I have men downstairs that will be arriving any moment to take your heads."

"Also dead," said Pepe.

Abbo furled his brow. "You play. You will see."

"The tall one, the two skinny men, the one with the scar? Dead, dead, dead, and dead, and your driver, too. Oui, he is also dead."

"That is impossible," said Abbo.

"No," said Pepe. "Far from impossible." He produced a knife from the inside of his jumpsuit. "I cut their throats one by one."

Abbo jolted himself from the bed, away from Pepe.

Cameron lifted his MP-5, "Ah, ah. Stay right there."

Abbo peered up at Cameron, judging the next action, and then relaxed back onto the headboard, his attempt to scramble failed.

"You are the assassins," said Abbo. He straightened his back and then cleared his throat. Abbo's head drooped around to Cameron, "You. You are a spy from the CIA, or one of the others from above, maybe?"

"No," said Cameron. "I'm just the wrong fella to mess with."

"Seems you hijacked the wrong yacht," said Pepe, "and took the wrong girl."

Abbo began to lean forward, "I don't know what you are talking about."

In a flash, Pepe raised his MP-5 high and then thrust his elbow back into the chest of the captive giant. The headboard cracked loudly as Abbo's weight burst back.

Abbo yelled up at Pepe, "What do you want with me?"

"Where is Christine?" asked Pepe.

"Who is Christine? I do not know who you are talking about."

Pepe's stout body twisted and his knee flew up into Abbo's chest, planting the warlord further into the bed.

Abbo lifted his hands to cover himself, his eyes wide, "Really, I do not know what you are talking about. I do not know about a yacht or this girl Christine."

Pepe swung the muzzle of the MP-5 back toward Abbo's face.

"Hold on," said Cameron. "We are talking about the Kalinihta. Demetrius Stratos' yacht you hijacked and took to your compound when you kidnapped his son Nikos and Christine, the woman that was with him. We have Nikos and we want Christine."

"You fools," said Abbo. "I did no such thing."

"What are you talking about?" asked Cameron.

"You have been deceived. Dada is the kidnapper. It was him that kidnapped my son and took him to this compound you speak of. The compound belongs to Dada."

"What are you saying?" asked Pepe.

"I have nothing that far north. Dada took that compound from the Merca when he drove them out. Why would I hijack that yacht? I have no quarrel with Demetrius Stratos. I have been dealing with him for years."

Cameron shook his head, "You're lying."

"No, no," said Abbo. "This is about money."

"What money?"

"The waste disposal money. That is what Dada wants. Demetrius charges one thousand euros per ton to dispose of toxic waste created by companies across Europe. For five euros per ton, the National Volunteer Coast Guard allows his ships to dump millions of tons of the waste. They dump far out in Somali waters. Demetrius pays me, and then pockets the difference. Why would I ruin all of this?" Abbo gestured his hand around the suite. "This is that scheming Dada. Dada is in London to rework the deal for the Somali Marines."

Alastair had returned and was at the foot of the bed, "He is lying to save himself."

"I am not lying. Dada has made a fool of you to win the deal with Demetrius and to take me out at the same time. My spies tell me he tries to get double increase. He wants everything. He is the one that sent you, is he not?"

"Why do you say that?" asked Cameron.

Wounded, Abbo lowered his voice, "Maybe you work for Dada? Maybe you were the ones who took my son? What have you done with him? Have you killed Feizel, killed my son?"

"He's lying," said Alastair.

"He's not," said Pepe.

"When is the last time you saw your son?" asked Cameron.

"I have not seen my son in weeks. He is not content to stay here. He is young and travels through Europe with the young people, where the young people dance. He was last in Ibiza when I spoke with him, then he disappeared."

"Disappeared? What do you mean?" asked Cameron.

"We always talk, every few days. Then nothing. He did not use his credit cards. No one had seen him. I was told he had been kidnapped and taken to the compound in Kismayu. By the time my men were able to get there, the compound had been burnt to the ground. Was that you?"

"Yes," said Cameron. "We liberated Stratos' yacht and crew from the compound."

Abbo stretched his neck tall, "Did you see my son? Do you know what that dog did with him?"

"Not everyone was there," said Pepe. "That is why we are here."

"Then I must go to London," said Abbo. "I know now what he is up to. I will set things right with Demetrius and I will torture that dog Dada to find out where my son is."

"Your son is dead," said Alastair.

"What?" asked Abbo.

"Feizel was in on the deal to screw over his old man," said Alastair. "The heir to the throne. Just didn't play out like he thought."

Abbo's eyes began to blaze red, "Now you lie!"

Alastair continued, "He had a gun when we arrived. What kidnapper would give their hostage a gun?"

"Where is he? What have you done?"

"He is dead," said Alastair. He nodded toward Pepe. "My friend shot him in the head."

Abbo shouted a guttural scream, "No, this cannot be!" He threw his outstretched hand up toward Pepe's neck, his wrists and fingers gnarled in the air, prepared to mangle. Pepe's knees buckled as he dropped back to dodge the lunging warlord. Pepe squeezed his trigger as the warlord soared toward him.

Abbo convulsed in the air, riddled by the stings of the MP-5 submachine gun, before falling twisted on the bed, less half his skull, which now plastered the face of the headboard.

"Why did you have to go and say that?" asked Cameron.

"You really think he was going to forget about us?" said Alastair. "He was going to hunt us down for what we did today alone, and once he found out the truth about Feizel." Alastair shrugged, "Well."

CHAPTER 39
ABBO'S SUITE, BURJ KHALIFA LEVEL 105, DUBAI

The door of the suite boomed in thwacks and thuds, the hollers of the men on the other side escalating in accordance with their impatience.

"Sounds like they really want to get in," said Cameron.

Alastair was stowing all of the loose gear back into the duffels. He glanced out into the night past the glass wall. "We have less than a minute to wait for our cue."

Pepe was setting the final charges around the edges of the glass. "Will that be enough time? As soon as Abbo's men figure out the card reader's shorted they are going to take that door."

"They will have to have great luck trying," said Alastair. " I checked the lock when I sent Antoinette out to the corridor, that door should hold."

Cameron zipped the front of his jumpsuit, "This fits, and I get a logo as well."

"They came in a set," said Alastair. "You know, Pepe, if you would have really killed all of his downstairs men like you told him we would not be in a rush."

"I would have enjoyed the task," said Pepe. "You were the one that said we should minimize risk by manipulating the camera system. You should have started the fountain sooner."

Alastair stopped and shifted his gaze to Pepe. "I triggered the remote as soon as I bloody well could, thank you. I think all of Dubai is going to appreciate this unscheduled performance." Alastair resumed zipping the duffels. "You should take a look down at the extravaganza."

"Hmm," said Pepe. "Magnific."

"You're damn right," said Alastair. "They haven't used those extreme shooters since the opening ceremony."

"They really shoot the water fifty stories in the air?" asked Cameron, adjusting his harness.

"With percussion as loud as thunder. When those babies go off this whole building, that entire mall, hell, the whole city, is going to shake. It will be great. Except..."

Pepe was adjusting his harness as well. Without looking at Alastair, he asked, "Except what?"

"I said they haven't been used since the opening ceremony."

"So?" asked Pepe.

"When I went out on the lake this afternoon to calibrate them, they registered as engaged on the control screen."

"That's fine then," said Cameron.

"Well, that only means they are calibrated for the performance and registering. If they are not set up to receive pressure or something goes wrong, this may not work."

"So then the world knows we are here?" asked Pepe.

"We reduce the element of diversion," said Alastair.

"No matter," said Cameron, "we're leaving. Do you hear them out there? They're rabid."

"No worries. There would have to be—" Alastair abruptly paused as the yelling suddenly escalated, flooding the suite beyond the master bedroom, "A secondary mechanism. There would have to be a secondary mechanism. How did we miss that?"

"We need to go now," said Cameron. "The bolts on this door won't hold them long."

Abbo's soldiers began thumping the bedroom door.

"All good," said Alastair. "The music is about to crescendo and then we make our exit. Three small percussions, then the two larger ones. Ready yourselves."

"What music?" asked Pepe.

"You cannot hear the music from here?" asked Alastair. From beyond the glass wall, they heard a muffled boom. "That's one. You'd better back up."

From inside the suite they heard furniture now thudding against the door.

"That's two."

Pepe held the trigger in his hand.

"And three, get ready, Pepe."

The panels in the center of the bedroom door began to break inward, yet the door stayed secure in the frame.

Alastair's focus was intense. His eyes went vacant as he distinguished the outside concussions from the rounds the men beyond the door were firing into the locks.

Alastair yelled, "Now!"

Pepe flipped the charge in sync with the sound of thunder from the extreme shooters of the Dubai fountain below. The glass wall disintegrated into the Dubai night, high above the lake.

At that same moment, Abbo Mohammed's men broke the door to the master bedroom free from the reinforced bolts.

Pepe, Cameron, and Alastair thrust themselves into the void adjacent to the tower As Somali soldiers poured into the dead warlord's room.

Pepe, Cameron, and Alastair separated quickly on launch, then tossed their chutes out, their canopies pulled up and open. The soldiers raced to the perch of the now open level. Alastair's voice tinned in Pepe's ear, "Now, Pepe."

Pepe squeezed the second igniter.

To the left of the three commandos, eruptions of fuchsia hued water towered upward, high above the other buildings around them, accompanied by thunder. The series of charges set throughout the suite during the sweep exploded in a cascade, propelling the unprepared soldiers from the open ledge.

Alastair pointed a green laser toward a darkened parking area to the far right of the fountain spectacle. As the three drew closer, a fluorescent green glow stick appeared, first waving, then still. Using the light of the glow stick as their guide, the three honed on their target.

The heat of the desert enveloped Cameron.

Though the next steps were clear—go to London and to Dada—that left little relief. Their plan was to BASE jump with a fourth. A fourth that was supposed to be held by Abbo Mohammed, and she wasn't here.

Cameron adjusted the lines of his canopy to swing himself around and into alignment with the green glow stick. Cameron heard a whizzing close behind, another, and then two concussions filled the air. Hundreds of amber and indigo lights filled the heavens above him.

"What the hell," said Cameron.

Into his ear, Alastair responded, "The fireworks are beginning to erupt."

"Fireworks? Are you nuts?" Another whiz shot behind Cameron, followed by another pop, resulting this time in a magenta sky.

"I didn't think they would turn on," said Alastair. "I didn't put them in when I created the show protocol. There must be an automatic override."

"An automatic override?" asked Cameron.

"Don't worry. They're farther away than they seem and we are about to touch down."

The next rockets went up with a swish. "Oh, dear,"

said Alastair.

"Is that what I think?" asked Pepe.

"Hold on," said Cameron.

The sky above lit amber again, this time to the sound of popcorn popping, and then the rain began. Surrounded by the pouring lit remnants of giant fire blossoms, the three were ready for the silks to degrade and for airspeed to rapidly increase. None of those things happened. The lightshow was farther away then they perceived, an illusion.

The dim parking lot became illuminated as they dropped close. The only vehicle, a vintage VW van, was parked to the side. The three touched down as they had countless times before and in the same motion, began to gather their gear. Rehan, the twelve-year-old boy from the Marmoom Camel track, was waiting next to the open doors of the van. He scurried over to the center of the parking area, scooped up the glow stick, and then buried the light in his pocket. Rehan then ran over to Pepe and, with two hands and a heave of a lift, clutched his duffel. "Let me help you stow everything in the lorry, Sayyed. I have the water and food you requested. Where is the other?"

"We have to make another stop," said Cameron. "C'mon, let's stow everything into the van and get out of here."

CHAPTER 40
PARIS COUNTRYSIDE, FIFTEEN YEARS BEFORE

The voyeuristic glances of Christine, stolen through the Citroen's rearview mirror, pleased Cameron. In the backseat was innocent bliss. She had wrapped the chocolate lab in her scarf, cradling the puppy as she would a baby, and now soothed her tiny brown bundle with a maternal voice.

"You are such a cute baby," said Christine. "Are you a cute baby? Yes, you are."

The miniature muzzle poked up to reach Christine's chin, so she folded herself toward him, giggling while his tongue basted her neck. "Such nice kisses. You are a darling little one." Her words appeared to encourage him to eagerly devour his new mistress with a tongue lapping that paired with her further laughter.

"You have a new love," said Cameron.

"Isn't he beautiful? What should we name him?"

"What would you like?"

"Oh, I already love him so much," said Christine. "Maybe little Cameron."

"Are you serious?"

Christine shifted her eyes up from the pup to the mirror, "Don't sound like a grump. You will hurt his feelings. I would not name this little darling a grumpy man's name."

"Hey, I am hurt."

"You are not. Besides, I want him to keep me company when you are away, not remind me of how much I miss you."

Cameron had no response to this. His time between missions had diminished with each assignment. His career was unique, allusive, and one he was unable to share with Christine. He could not fool himself. Not too much time would pass before two to four week stints would turn to three and then six month operations. There were operatives he was aware of that had been in the field for years. His special talents had advanced him beyond one and done direct action missions. Christine's opportunities were advancing as well, having traveled twice to Asia and once to Mexico already this year. A time would soon come when the few brief, fleeting days of the calendar, days when the two lovers could be together, would no longer intersect.

"I know," said Christine. "He looks like a Moby." She dipped her chin and the lab lapped at her again. "You like that name? Moby."

"What is a Moby?" asked Cameron.

"He is a Moby."

"Doesn't Moby mean immense, enormous, like the whale?"

Christine pushed her nose down into Moby, "Vous avez un immense amour? Yes, you do, a Moby heart." Christine glanced up to where Cameron's eyes would meet her, "He has an immense love like you."

Whether the warmth came from her green eyes or from the words she chose, Christine stoked a fire within Cameron's core that burned throughout his limbs and straight up the back of his neck, stiffening his skull with the anxiety of a small boy. She dropped one brow ever so slightly. A quiver shot through him, a nauseous jolt that forced Cameron to widen his eyes and pull his attention toward the road.

"We may still have some luck," said Cameron. He lowered his head to look out and beyond the bonnet of the Citroen. "The sun has broken through."

"Marvelous, we can still have our picnic."

CAMERON KINCAID RETURNS IN
THE SOMALI DECEPTION
EPISODE III

ABOUT THE AUTHOR

Daniel Arthur Smith is the author of the international bestsellers *THE CATHARI TREASURE, THE SOMALI DECEPTION,* and a few other novels and short stories.

He was raised in Michigan and graduated from Western Michigan University where he studied meta-physics, cognitive science, philosophy, and comparative religion. He began his career as a bartender, barista, poetry house proprietor, teacher and then became a technologist and futurist for the Fortune 100 across the Americas and Europe.

Daniel has traveled to over 300 cities in 22 countries, residing in Los Angeles, Kalamazoo, Prague, Crete, and now writes in Manhattan where he lives with his wife and young sons.

For more information, visit **danielarthursmith.com**

STAY IN THE LOOP

Following your favorite authors on Facebook, Twitter, or other social media has become a sketchy business. Facebook and other companies block authors from conversing regularly with readers unless they are willing to cough up BIG BUX to 'promote' every post. To make sure you are receiving the latest updates, freebies, and stories on everything in the Daniel Arthur Smith universe you have to join his email newsletter. As a subscriber, you'll receive early Advance Review Copies (ARCS) of all of Daniel's books and stories... for free! In addition to all of that, Daniel regularly gives away lots of other loot like signed books and posters, so make certain that you are subscribed.